Praise for *Ci*

Winner of the RAI Special Merit Award

◄o►

"A brilliant account of contemporary Irish teenage life."
Sunday Business Post

"An authentic voice . . . "
The Irish Times

"A great novel, full of the vitality of adolescent angst, the reality of never being understood."
Evening Press

"A humdinger of a book."
Sunday World

THE DOOR

THE DOOR

MARGRIT CRUICKSHANK

BEACON BOOKS

POOLBEG

Published 1996
by Poolbeg Press Ltd
123 Baldoyle Industrial Estate
Dublin 13, Ireland

The Publishers gratefully acknowledge the support of The Arts Council.

"The Door" by Miroslav Holub reprinted by permission of Bloodaxe Books Ltd from: Poems Before & After (Bloodaxe Books, 1990).

Extracts from *The Official Politically Correct Dictionary and Handbook* and *Sex and Dating, The Official Politically Correct Guide* by Beard & Cerf reprinted by permission of HarperCollins *Publishers* Ltd.

A catalogue record for this book is available from the British Library.

ISBN 1 85371 617 0

Cover illustration by Peter Hannon
Cover design by Poolbeg Group Services Ltd
Set by Poolbeg Group Services Ltd in Times 11/13.5
Printed by The Guernsey Press Ltd,
Vale, Guernsey, Channel Islands.

Also by Margrit Cruickshank

SKUNK and the Ozone Conspiracy
SKUNK and the Splitting Earth
SKUNK and the Nuclear Waste Plot
SKUNK and the Freak Flood Fiasco
Circling the Triangle
Anna's Six Wishes
Liza's Lamb

Published by Poolbeg

My thanks are due to Jenny and Kirsten (who read the manuscript), to Rebecca, Don, Philip and Clare (some of whose suggestions were particularly unhelpful) - and especially to Andrew.

And also, of course, to Bernard and Mary at Annaghmakerrig.

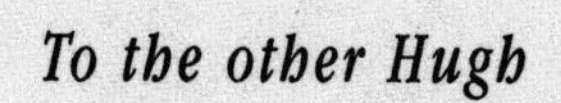

To the other Hugh

Contents

Chapter 1	1
Chapter 2	6
Chapter 3	10
Chapter 4	13
Chapter 5	21
Chapter 6	28
Chapter 7	33
Chapter 8	38
Chapter 9	45
Chapter 10	49
Chapter 11	56
Chapter 12	64
Chapter 13	67
Chapter 14	75
Chapter 15	79
Chapter 16	85
Chapter 17	94
Chapter 18	100
Chapter 19	107
Chapter 20	114
Chapter 21	117
Chapter 22	124
Chapter 23	131
Chapter 24	139
Chapter 25	144
Chapter 26	154
Chapter 27	159
Chapter 28	164
Chapter 29	167

Chapter 1

All the world's a stage,
And all the men and women merely players.
Shakespeare, *As You Like It*

Write an extended essay on what YOU got out of Transition Year. What new interests did you take up? What did you learn? Did you find it a positive experience?

There's a price to pay for everything, even a doss year at school: we might have guessed Ms Blenchley, our Year Leader, would stick us with a mini-thesis on the thing. OK, here we go. *New interests: girls. Learnt: French kissing. Was it a positive experience? What do you think, Ms Blenchley?* If only I had the guts.

Actually, that's not a hundred miles from the truth. New interest: Rachel. Learnt: a lot. Was it a positive experience? Ah, there's the rub, as Shakespeare said somewhere.

And Shakespeare was where it all started. Gleeson was directing the Transition Year play, *Romeo and Juliet,* and we were all in it: Dave was playing Romeo, Marie-Claire Juliet, Rachel the nurse and I was helping backstage. If someone had told me then that, by the end of the year, I'd become interested in Rachel Cross, I'd have referred him to the men (and women; yes, indeed, Rachel *has* been a formative experience) in white coats.

Anyway, the four of us were walking down to our respective bus stops after one of the last rehearsals for the play. It was February, the wind was howling down from Greenland and the Wicklow mountains were white.

Rachel was sounding off as usual: "He shouldn't be allowed to get away with it!"

"OK," Dave said. "Agreed. So what do you suggest we do?"

"Something. Report him. I don't know."

"Report him to who? The Blenchley? He's a teacher – she'll take his side."

"Not necessarily. It's sexual harassment, that's what it is. Even Ms Blenchley has to be against that."

Marie-Claire sighed. "Dave's right, Rache. There's no point. Teachers always stick together."

"It's people who think the way you do that's got the world in the mess it's in." Rachel hitched her bag more firmly on to her shoulder. "Of *course* there's a point. *Someone* has to stop Gleeson."

We were discussing an incident at the rehearsal we'd just come from. Marie-Claire and Dave had been going over the scene, at the end of Act I, where Romeo is trying to get off with Juliet and gives this mega-complicated speech so he can con Juliet into letting him kiss her.

"We have to do *something*." Rachel, typically, just wouldn't let up. "I mean, he practically knocked Dave down today, just to get a chance to drool all over you."

"He didn't 'drool all over me'. Don't exaggerate, Rache. He was only showing Dave how to say the lines. I mean, he can't help being the way he is."

"You're right. He can't." I gave Dave a shove. "We just have to put up with him."

Dave grinned and shoved me back.

"No," Marie-Claire said. "I mean Creepy Chris. He probably doesn't even know what he's doing, the effect it has on people."

"Yeah. And maybe all the guys who go around raping and murdering women don't know what *they* are doing either?"

"*All* the guys?" Dave asked, raising an eyebrow.

"Come on, Rache," Marie-Claire objected. "Calm down. He's not *that* bad."

"No?" Rachel put on a simpering voice: "'He's a good boy, really, officer. It's just a phase he's going through.'"

"Gleeson is a smarmy git," Dave announced, pulling up the hood of his anorak against the February wind. "I agree with you on that."

"He's not my favourite teacher either," I said. "But you have to admit he's an OK director. The play is going to be good, despite your pathetic acting this afternoon."

"*My* pathetic acting? I was psyching myself up, getting ready to meet the beautiful Marie-Claire-stroke-Juliet for the first time in my short-but-exciting life, willing to fondle her hand all day if necessary for the sake of art . . ."

"Well, thank *you,* noble sir," Marie-Claire fluttered her eyelashes and dropped Dave a demure curtsey.

". . . and he didn't give me a chance. He just grabbed your hand and, as Rachel said, practically spewed up his dinner over it."

"Not what I said. But it'll do. He's a total scumbag. Thank God the play goes on next week. If I had to listen to him for much longer, 'interpreting' the love scenes with his *doubles entendres* . . ."

"His what?"

"Buy a dictionary . . . and his dirty little jokes, I'd end up sticking a rapier into him. And all you guys giggle happily along. I thought you were meant to be New Men, your generation."

"Nah. Recycled old ones, really."

"Recycled? From what? Old egg cartons?"

"Ha, ha."

Marie-Claire tried to change the subject. "Now that the play's nearly over, have any of you thought what we're going to do next? As an extra-curricular activity, I mean."

Dave put an arm round her shoulders and gave her a squeeze. "I've a few ideas," he said huskily.

She bashed her bag into his shins and pulled away from him.

"You're as bad as that perv Gleeson," Rachel snorted. "You men only ever think of one thing."

Dave leered at her. "How did you guess? Are you offering to give it, me?"

All Rachel gave him was a look that would have frozen hot chocolate.

Marie-Claire blushed. "Will you stop messing," she said. "And I'm serious. We have to find another interest for after the play. Do any of you have any ideas?"

"After the play? You mean this hell is one day going to end? Are you telling me there's light at the end of the tunnel?"

"Shut it, Dave. You're having yourself a great time," I told him. "And Marie-Claire's right. The Blenchley's not going to let us just hang loose after this. Remember, 'we need a continuous succession of interests to expand our minds in this year free from the pressures of academic work'."

"We could do an evening class," Marie-Claire suggested. "Or take up a musical instrument?"

Both these ideas had been put forward by Ms Blenchley at

the beginning of the year, but nobody reminded Marie-Claire of this. "Don't make it the piano," I advised her. "You might hurt your back."

"What? Oh. Very funny, Hugh."

"We should form a band," Dave said firmly. "I mean, Hugh and I play guitar and you girls . . ."

"Could be your backing group?" Rachel hitched up the long skirt she was wearing to reveal short plump legs in black tights. She kicked a foot in the air. "I was wrong, you're *worse* than Creepy Chris."

"I was going to say that Marie-Claire could sing . . ."

"Of course. She has the looks!"

"And you could . . . I don't know. How about drums?"

"How about them?"

"I know a fellow who might sell us a set cheap."

"Forget it," Rachel told him.

And then Dave's bus came round the corner and he had to leg it and that was that.

That conversation was where it all started. Do I regret what came after? No, Ms Blenchley. I don't think that I do.

Chapter 2

Twenty-one of the first twenty-three U.S. astronauts who flew on space missions were either an only child or were first-born sons.

Ma wasn't in when I got home. I went into the kitchen, took three white rolls out of the freezer and defrosted them in the microwave. I filled one with butter and crisps, the second with ham, chutney, peanuts and salad, and the third with banana and raspberry jam: starters, main course and sweet. A man needs sustenance after a hard day at school.

Heaping the whole lot on to a plate with a glass of milk, I went into the den, switched on the television, put my feet up on the couch and watched Jerry outwit Tom on children's television. Tom fell out of a top floor window into a concrete mixer. It churned a couple of times, then spat him out like a cannonball. He flew through the air, crashed against the garden fence and landed, a furious feline statue, on the gatepost just as Ma's key grated in the front door.

I took my feet off the couch and tried, unsucessfully, to hide my plate. Too late.

"Hugh! How often do I have to tell you you're not to eat in

the drawing room? Why do I have to keep repeating things one million times?"

I smiled up at her. "And it's nice to see you too, Mother dear. Yes, I did have a good day at school. And how was yours?"

"Lousy. And it has certainly not been improved by coming home and finding my one and only son dragging food all through the house and stuffing himself so full he'll leave half his dinner on his plate. You're not a baby any more, you know, that needs feeding every three hours. You're supposed to be almost a man."

"Thanks for that 'almost', Ma. I am touched."

"You know what I mean. And, if you want to be treated like an adult, behave like one. Take that plate out into the kitchen. And pick up all the crumbs you've dropped on the carpet. Honest, Hugh. You think I have nothing better to do than clean up after you all the time."

I picked up most of the crumbs and stood up. "You like it. You know you do. Makes you feel wanted."

Ma sighed. "Oh, get out of here. Haven't you any homework to do?"

"Nope. We're in Transition Year, remember? We had three free periods today: I got it all done in school."

She plumped up the cushions I'd been leaning against. "Transition Year. A waste of time, I call it. You don't seem to do any work at all."

"Ah but we do. We have Life Skills and Media Studies and Drama and . . ."

She grinned. "OK. Then practise your life skills by clearing away the mess I'm sure you've made in the kitchen and peel some potatoes for me." She gestured at the television, where Tom had burst out of his concrete casing and was shinning up the drainpipe to get at Jerry again. "Or is this part of your media studies?"

"Could be." Jerry banged the window down on Tom's fingers and Tom plummeted slowly through space to make a spread-eagled hole in the lawn. "Note how the aggressor, Tom, is actually the victim. Maybe I should do psychology when I leave school. I mean, it's so obvious: the strong manipulated by the weak. Men *think* they've got the upper hand but, in reality, they're bashed about at every turn by girlfriends, wives and mothers. Especially mothers."

"Really? How fascinating." She turned off the television. "On your bike, lad. Potatoes. You've just got time to make your one and only speciality: there's spring onions in the vegetable rack. I bought some steak for dinner; potatoes *au gratin* would go well with that. I might even open a bottle of wine."

"See what I mean?" I edged past her out of the room. "Oh for the good old days when a woman's place was in the kitchen and a real man wouldn't be seen dead in an apron. I was born into the wrong generation."

She took a swipe at me and missed.

Dave came round after dinner.

"About this band. What do you think?"

"I dunno. It's OK your saying you can get hold of a drum kit cheap, but who's going to pay for it? Not to mention amps and all the rest?"

"You parents are loaded. Why not ask for amps for your birthday or something?"

"Maybe because my birthday's not till September? Or maybe because I just don't want them."

"Come on, it'd be great. We could enter the Battle of the Bands. Maybe even win a recording session. Just imagine . . ." Dave swept a hand through the air in front of him, narrowly missing the Mr Happy mug I keep on my desk to hold pens and things in. "Our name up in lights at the Point Depot, recording sessions in London, touring the States . . ."

"In your dreams."

"Yeah, well. If you don't dream, you'll never get anywhere."

"Sure."

"We could get part-time work," Dave went on. "I mean, that's another of the 'opportunities' of this fantastic-amazing year. Earn enough to buy the drums and the rest of the stuff."

"You do that."

"Aw, come on. Show some enthusiasm."

"Why? I don't feel any. And the girls didn't seem too keen, either."

"Fine. We do it without them. There's plenty of lads around."

I hesitated.

Dave grinned. "Don't tell me you're falling in love? *Alas, poor Romeo, he is already dead! stabbed with a white wench's black eye; shot through the ear with a love-song; the very pin of his heart cleft with the blind bow-boy's butt-shaft.* It's only a play, remember."

"But isn't all the world a stage?" I countered.

"Aye, marry, sir, it is. So which of the wenches dost thou pine for, forsooth?"

"I don't pine."

"No? Do you larch then? Or beech? Or even hawthorn?"

"Just get this straight," I told him. "I don't fancy anyone. And the reason I'm not into spending the rest of this year messing with a band is because it'll be just that: messing. This is the last year we won't have exam pressure. We ought to do something really good with it."

"A band would be really good," Dave muttered as he picked up his jacket and made for the door.

Maybe it would have been. It would certainly have meant a lot less hard work and would have got us into a lot less trouble.

But, if we'd started a band, I might never have got to know Rachel better. And I'm glad I did. Or most of the time I'm glad, anyhow.

Chapter 3

Acting was once considered so frivolous an occupation that authorities in Virginia, in 1610, forbade the immigration of actors from England.

The dress rehearsal for the play took place a couple of days later. It was a disaster. Most of the actors spoke (or, more to the point, didn't speak) as if they'd only been given their lines that morning; and as for knowing where to stand and what to do . . .

Eventually Gleeson called a break. He gathered us around him: Jesus on the hilltop dishing out bread and fishes. Only it wasn't food he was dispensing.

"In case some of you hadn't noticed, this play is going on tomorrow evening, not next year, or even next century," he informed us. "Your doting mums and dads will be hanging on your every word (that is, assuming you learn some between now and then). Not to mention your even-more-doting significant other persons, as I gather they are called these days, who may well come to listen to what the Bard actually wrote, some of them having the play for their exams next term, and not simply to lust after your splendid bodies."

"Why doesn't he take a running jump at himself," Rachel muttered to the rest of us.

"Did you say something, Rachel? Or were you just practising your feminine wiles?"

"Sod off," Rachel hissed between clenched teeth.

Gleeson smiled. "OK, boys and girls. Take five. And let's hope things improve when we start again."

Having watched the cast mangling the play from the lighting box, I must admit I had a certain sympathy for him. "What an excruciatingly bloody shambles, darlings," I lisped to Dave and the girls. "You're going to be here absolutely all night, sweeties, unless something comes together soon."

"Watch it, O'Connor," Dave threatened. "Just because you're too chicken to go on the stage yourself . . ."

"Squawk, squawk, squawk, squawk," I clucked.

"Dress rehearsals are always dire," Marie-Claire said hopefully. "It's traditional. Everyone will be OK tomorrow night."

"Everyone? Even Stuart Kinsella?"

"He *almost* knows his lines."

"Betwixt 'almost' and 'actually' lies a chasm, as Shakespeare might have said," I told her. "You remind me of my mother."

"She does?" Dave grinned. "Either you need glasses, or Freud's wiser than I thought. You'd better watch out, Marie-Claire. Keep well clear of a man with an Oedipus complex."

I punched him. Marie-Claire looked embarrassed. "I wonder if Shakespeare had to put up with bad actors too?" she asked quickly.

"Probably. But I doubt if he ever used anybody as bad as this lot. Present company excepted, of course."

"Of course."

Rachel watched Gleeson leaning against the wall of the

gym, chatting up a group of girls. They were dressed as gentlewomen of Verona. The low-cut bodices of their costumes were . . . well, low-cut. And Gleeson was obviously enjoying the view.

"That man is a lech. Just look at him."

"He's only talking to Aoife and June and the others."

Rachel sighed. "Marie-Claire, if you saw the Big Bad Wolf walking through the woods, you'd go up to him and pat him and say 'good doggie', and spend the rest of the day trying to find a home for him. You're impossible."

"I just like to see the best in people. You like to see the worst."

"With Creepy Chris that's not difficult." Rachel scowled. "There must be a way to get at him."

Gleeson unstuck himself from the gym wall. "OK, gang. Break's over. Back to the grindstone. And see if some of you at least can remember your lines. It would be nice if you could also look as if you *understood* what you're saying, but maybe I'm asking too much. Just try to remember that you're supposed to be real people, act they ever so weirdly, not stuffed glove puppets."

The cast groaned and dragged themselves to their feet. I went back to the lighting box and the rehearsal resumed.

Chapter 4

> To help managers learn more about the legal perils of close dancing and other problem areas such as "hugging" and "kissing under the mistletoe," Mr Goldstein has narrated a videotape entitled *How to Prevent Sexual Harassment Lawsuits*, which his public-spirited firm generously makes available to clients and nonclients alike for the nominal fee of $79.95 per copy.
>
> *Sex and Dating, The Official Politically Correct Guide*, Beard & Cerf, HarperCollins

Marie-Claire's optimism was rewarded. The first night of the play wasn't as disastrous as I'd feared, although we were all pretty nervous – and the jeers and whistles from the audience didn't help.

We improved each night. In fact, by the last performance, even Stuart Kinsella knew most of his lines. Apart, that is, from his big speech at the end.

"Did you hear him?" Dave crowed at the party in my house afterwards. "He was brilliant. 'Juliet, there dead, was husband to that Romeo . . . No, I mean *Romeo*, there dead, was husband to that Romeo. . . I mean, husband to that *Juliet* . . .'"

"Oh, *that* Juliet!" Rachel sniggered.

The four of us were in the kitchen, sampling the beer Dad

kept in the back of the fridge. Dave waved his beer-can in the air. "The rest was pure magic. I wish I'd had a tape recorder. How did it go? 'I married them and then you, like, went and chucked Romeo out of the city and, you know, tried to get Juliet to shack up with that guy Paris, so she, like, takes the sleeping pills and he thinks she's dead and kills Paris and then he kills himself, so she, like, knifes herself and, if you want to know anything more about it, ask her nurse.' He ought to be writing notes on the play."

"I'm glad to see you're enjoying yourselves." Gleeson appeared in the doorway, a glass of punch in his hand. "Well done, all of you. It was not perhaps the greatest performance of the bard in the last three centuries, but I think we managed to carry it off." He put his free arm round Marie-Claire and gave her a squeeze. "Due mainly to Juliet here and her Romeo."

Marie-Claire went scarlet and eased herself out from under his grasp.

"Are you having an orgy in here? Can anyone join in?" Gleeson obviously thought he was being ultra cool. Why is it some adults never realize how sad they are when they try to pretend they're one of us?

Dave, who had hidden his can behind his back, swivelled to face the sink and ran the hot tap. "We're just doing a bit of tidying up, sir."

"Ah yes," Gleeson said, looking round the four of us with a leer. "So you are. Well, don't let me stop you." He smiled and disappeared again.

"Sir?" I asked Dave, raising an eyebrow.

"Well, he caught me off-guard. If they discover there's beer in here, everyone will want some."

"What a slimeball!" Rachel muttered. "What made you invite him, Hugh?"

"I couldn't very well not. He did direct the play, after all."

"Huh."

Marie-Claire yawned. "God, I'm wrecked. I suppose it's the anticlimax or something, now that it's all over. It's like we've been doing nothing but the play for months. It's been a laugh, though." She turned to the rest of us. "Maybe we should join a drama society or something. What do you think?"

"I am never going to to get involved in a play again, ever, for the rest of my life," Dave said vehemently. "Not if someone paid me a fortune."

"Really?" Rachel asked sweetly. "I thought you'd do anything for money? And I'm surprised all that applause hasn't gone to your head."

Dave made a rude sign at her. "It's all 'come here, go there, say this, do that . . .' It's even worse than school. Forget it. Tonight, we're supposed to be having a good time."

"Maybe we should leave the rest of the beer for Dad and go back to join the others," I suggested.

"Do we have to? I don't know what's in that drink your Ma's provided, but I think I prefer an honest pint."

"Are you making accusations about Ma's famous, non-alcoholic punch?"

Rachel, who had brought a glass of punch into the kitchen with her, held it up to the light, like a housewife examining stains in a washing-powder advertisement. "*Non*-alcoholic?" she asked.

"It was, anyway. It's nothing to do with me, if something's got into it since."

"Of course," Rachel murmured, taking another sip.

"I *am* responsible for the music, though. So I suggest we go back to the party. I might even put on something nice and romantic, so that Romeo and Juliet here can get it together at last and give our play a happier ending."

Marie-Claire blushed and Dave glared as I shepherded them back into the sitting-room. I put a slow blues number on the stereo. "There you are, then. Music to kiss to. *If music be the food of love, play on;* though that's another play."

"You're as pathetic as Gleeson," Rachel muttered, but she allowed me to pull her out into the centre of the room for a dance.

Needless to say, we didn't kiss. Rachel was just a friend at that stage – or hardly even that. We'd only got to know her this year, and that was because of the play. She was in Marie-Claire's form which meant that the only subjects we shared were English and French; and, although I'd seen her in class (it would have been difficult not to, Rachel not being exactly shy when it came to voicing her opinions), she didn't do a lot for me. I went for blondes, for a start, and she was a redhead. OK, she had nice eyes – sort of tawny-green. A bit like our cat's, in fact. But I liked girls tall and thin, not short and . . . well, cuddly.

Secondly, militant feminists just weren't my type.

The party went well. I kept the music going, made sure nobody slipped upstairs and messed up the bedrooms (fortunately, it being a cast party, we had very few gatecrashers) and danced with most of the gentlewomen of Verona as well as with Rachel and Marie-Claire. None of the girls seemed to lust madly after my body, but you can't have everything.

Just before midnight, Rachel announced that she was leaving.

"She says she's walking home by herself," Marie-Claire complained. "She won't wait till my father gets here."

"I'll be *fine*," Rachel said impatiently. "Stop going on about it."

"Dad's coming for me at one. He won't mind dropping you off."

I looked at my watch. “Come on, Rache. Give it a bit longer – or do you turn into a pumpkin at the stroke of twelve? Will we have to go all round town tomorrow, asking strange women to try on glass slippers? I don’t know if I’d be up to it.”

Rachel smiled, but didn’t take off her coat.

“Can’t you wait for Dad?” Marie-Claire pleaded. “You shouldn’t walk home on your own. Not this late.”

“Stop fussing,” Rachel told her again. “I’ll be OK. And I definitely have to go now.” She turned to me. “Great party, Hugh. See you Monday.”

“What thou needest, fair damsel, is a knight in shining armour,” I found myself suggesting. I held out my arm. “Allow me to escort you. The exercise, as Dave was *just* about to tell me, will do me good.”

“You read my thoughts.”

“I’m *OK*,” Rachel insisted.

I know I’d had a few pints and, of course, the punch, but I must have drunk more than I realised because it suddenly mattered to me, mattered very much, that Rachel didn’t walk home on her own. Some primaeval macho-male-protector thing, maybe; though I’ve never seen myself as a macho male – and Rachel is the last female in the school you would think of protecting. Probably it was just pigheadedness. “Of course you’re OK,” I told her soothingly. “Come on, now. Say goodnight to these nice people and we’ll away.”

Marie-Claire laughed. “Goodnight, Rache. See you in school Monday.”

Rachel gave me a funny look. “Well, if you’re sure. But you don’t have to, you know. I am well able to walk home on my own.”

I didn’t doubt it.

The cold air outside sobered me up quickly enough but I enjoyed the walk, all the same. Well, most of it. It was a clear night, the moon was new and the stars were twinkling like an ad for the Milky Way. We pointed out constellations to each other and talked about the immensity of the universe, infinity, God: things like that. Then we talked a bit about the play.

That was where I made my mistake: it allowed Rachel to get on to her obsession with Gleeson. And it was an obsession. Definitely.

"He's not that bad," I argued with her. "I mean he's just a normal male. OK, as a teacher he sometimes says things he shouldn't. But then, so do a lot of them. He doesn't mean any harm by it."

"So it's his hormones, is it?"

"Yeah. Have you ever wondered why you have a problem with that?"

"Why *I* have a problem with it?"

By this time we had reached her gate. "Look," I said. "He's a sleaze, but he's not worth losing the head about. Forget him. You're going way over the top about this, you know that?"

"You sound like Marie-Claire. 'Night, Hugh. Thanks for seeing me home."

She let herself into the house. A light went on in the hall, then another one upstairs. I remember thinking that it was strange, that – the fact that her house was in complete darkness not long after midnight on a Saturday night. Her folks must go to bed very early, I told myself. They could at least have left a light on for her.

But that was as far as my thoughts went. By the time I got back to the party, I'd forgotten about her completely.

I looked for Dave. He was dancing with Marie-Claire, jumping around like a gerbil on speed. Marie-Claire was doing her own thing opposite him. She seemed amused.

Then, as I watched, Gleeson came up to them, grabbed Marie-Claire's hand and pulled her away from Dave. Dave just stood there, gawping. He took a step after them, stopped, shrugged, saw me and elbowed his way through the crowd.

"Did you see that? Talk about abuse of power! Just because he's a teacher, he thinks he can get away with murder. *I* was dancing with Marie-Claire!"

"Is that what you call it?"

"Wha'?" Dave glared round the room, trying to catch a glimpse of Gleeson.

"Is that what you call what you do? Dancing?"

"Shut it," Dave growled, still scouring the room. "There they are. Jesus, will you look at that!"

I looked. Gleeson's idea of dancing differed radically from Dave's. He was just as frantic, but instead of prancing around on his own, he involved his partner, pulling Marie-Claire towards him, pushing her away, twirling her around, swinging her towards him again. She seemed to be enjoying it.

"It's called jiving," I told Dave. "They used to do it in the sixties. My Ma and Da still do."

Dave went over to the stereo and pressed the stop button. The music died instantly. It was like the game we used to play at parties when we were little: musical statues. Everybody stopped dead and turned to stare at him.

"There will now be a short intermission," Dave announced.

As people moved threateningly towards him, I watched Gleeson and Marie-Claire. Gleeson was red-faced and sweating, sort of leaning on Marie-Claire and looking as if he was about to have a heart attack. She tried to move away. He kept leaning on her. Finally, she shoved him off her, her face almost as pink as his. He said something and put out a hand to stop her but she turned her back and pushed past the other people on the floor, looking flustered.

I went over to meet her. "You OK?" I asked. "What was going on over there?"

"Nothing. I was just dancing with Mr Gleeson."

"Why are you so upset, then?"

"I'm not upset."

Dave materialised at her elbow. "Put another tape on, Hugh, will you. The peasants are beginning to revolt." He took her arm. "Come on, Marie-Claire. Let me show you Hugh's conservatory."

The two of them disappeared, I put on more music, and the party resumed. Gleeson didn't seem put out: I saw him a few minutes later at the centre of the room, jiving away again (with one of the gentlewomen of Verona this time) while his carroty hair bounced furiously on top of his narrow head.

In first year, Dave and I took bets about whether Gleeson's hair was genuine or not. Dave said it was a hairpiece, I said it wasn't. Dave fell against him one day, accidentally-on-purpose, when Gleeson was sitting at his desk marking tests, and grabbed at the top of his head: "Sorry, sir. I felt dizzy. I thought I was going to fall over." Dave got detention and I won the money.

Now it looked as if Dave was about to get himself a girlfriend. And what was I about to get? Dragged out of bed the next morning, despite a blinding headache, to finish tidying up the mess (some of them had stayed behind to half-clean the place, but Ma was never a great believer in half-clean); and a lecture from Dad for letting people drink his beer.

Yes.

Chapter 5

Antioch Rules. A landmark collection of regulations governing sexual conduct named after Antioch College, in Yellow Springs, Ohio, where they were first instituted. The basic premise . . . is that no sexual act is permissible unless and until any party who might be called upon to participate has given her or his "willing and verbal consent."

Sex and Dating, The Official Politically Correct Guide,
Beard & Cerf, HarperCollins

Marie-Claire had obviously told Rachel about Gleeson's behaviour at the party. Rachel stormed into the canteen at lunchtime the next Monday and thumped her tray down on the table, scattering bits of salad all over Dave's *Hot Press*. "Something will have to be done about that perv!" she announced.

Marie-Claire sat down gingerly at the other side of the table, looking as if she'd been caught with an unexploded landmine and didn't know quite how to handle it. "He only asked me to dance with him, Rache. Calm down."

"The way you told it, he practically *forced* you to dance with him."

"Not really. It was just that he cut in on Dave . . ."

"Ah yes, *Dave*," I said. "And what did you two get up to in the conservatory on Saturday night?"

Marie-Claire giggled. "Miss Scarlet killed Colonel Mustard with the lead piping in the conservatory! It's years since I played *Cluedo*."

I winked at Rachel. "Known as avoiding the question."

Rachel wasn't amused. "I think we should go and see Franklin about him," she declared. "Creepy Chris, I mean. Are you lot coming with me?"

"Complain to the Head? About a teacher? You must be mad!"

Marie-Claire looked even more embarrassed. "Just leave it, Rache. It's not worth making a fuss about. I mean, I'm sure Mr Gleeson doesn't realize what a creep he is. He's harmless, really."

"Harmless!" Rachel snorted. "Are you happy to wait until he attacks some poor first year in the loos before you do anything about him?"

We all groaned.

"Come off it, Rachel," I said. "Get real."

"Feminists really piss me off sometimes," Dave told the ceiling.

"Honest, Rache. You're exaggerating. You can't be serious."

But Rachel didn't give up. "OK. Let me ask you a question, Marie-Claire. Were you comfortable with having to dance with him on Saturday night?"

"Were you comfortable . . ." Dave mimicked. "You sound like one of these women on the telly. Oprah Winfrey or whoever." He put on a posh, mincing voice: "Now, tell me, Miss Hannigan, how did you cope with this sex-maniac dragging you away from the only good-looking guy at the party last Saturday?"

"The only what?" I asked.

"It's not funny," Rachel insisted. "And it isn't just Saturday. Gleeson's always been a sleaze and people shouldn't have to put up with him. I mean, he always gets the girls with the shortest skirts to open the windows. And everybody knows that when you're writing something and he walks up and down between the desks, he's only trying to look down your front. Not to mention the remarks he makes. And the way he brushes against you any time he has the chance. He's a total scumbag. He has to be stopped."

"Maybe he's just a normal, red-blooded male?" I suggested innocently.

Rachel didn't rise to the bait. "I'm going to see Franklin anyway," she declared. "Who's coming with me?"

"Count me out," Dave muttered. "I see too much of Frankenstein as it is. I'm trying to keep a low profile."

"What about you, Marie-Claire? After all, you're the one that he's been bothering most, recently."

"I still think we should leave it. He's not *that* bad."

"Will you ever stop being a doormat and stick up for yourself? Listen, I'm going to make a formal complaint. It's sexual harassment, pure and simple. Are you coming or do I have to go on my own?"

Marie-Claire looked trapped. "OK, if you insist. I'll come with you. But really, there's no need."

"Hugh?"

I shrugged. "I agree with the others, it's not worth making an issue of. And anyway, if you're so worried about harassment, Rache, you're as bad as Gleeson, bullying Marie-Claire into coming with you."

Rachel looked surprised. "Am I bullying you?" she asked Marie-Claire. *Demanded* would be more the word, really.

"Don't be stupid," Marie-Claire said quickly.

"Drop it," Dave advised. "The two of you will only become marked men – sorry, Rachel, marked *women* – if you bother the Head with it. And you'll both end up looking really stupid. Frankenstein's never going to take your side against a teacher."

"Thanks, lads," Rachel said sarcastically. "So much for male support. But don't worry your poor little masculine heads about it, we'll be fine on our own. Won't we, Marie-Claire?"

Marie-Claire sighed. "OK, I've said I'll come with you. But I don't know what difference it'll make . . ."

The meeting didn't go well. The girls told us about it as we walked down the road after school, Marie-Claire still embarrassed about the whole thing, Rachel practically exploding with anger.

"'These are serious allegations you are making, Rachel . . .'" she mimicked Franklin's voice. "'Very serious. And everything you say is open to a completely innocent explanation. For example, if a woman teacher touched your hand when she was handing back an exercise, would you come to me about it?'"

"Well, would you?" I asked.

"Gleeson is not a woman teacher! And the man was so patronising! 'Can either of you give me one concrete example where Mr Gleeson's behaviour was sexually harassing?' And we'd just given him about a thousand!"

"He said he'd look into it," Marie-Claire reminded her.

"Yeah. And he also said that 'Mr Gleeson has always shown himself to be an excellent teacher and a responsible member of staff'. They'll all stick together. See if they won't."

"Well, don't say you weren't warned," Dave reminded her. "We knew you'd be wasting your time."

Rachel kicked a stone off the pavement into the middle of the road: Gleeson ought to have been glad it wasn't him she was kicking. "There must be a way to get him."

"The Get Gleeson Campaign!" Dave crowed. "I like it. Better than some of your other causes anyway. What are they all? Save the whale? Eliminate litter? Bring in the death penalty for smoking? Not to mention militant feminism: castrate all men!"

I grinned. Rachel threw me a filthy look.

"I've just finished a book about that," Marie-Claire said.

"About what? Castrating men?"

"Well, yes. It's called *After the Plague,* by someone called Jean Ure. It's all about a society a hundred years after the nuclear holocaust where women run everything and men are castrated."

"Fascinating," Dave and I murmured together.

"It was, too. They had a very peaceful society, no wars, no violence. But you were left in the end wondering if what they'd done was good or bad."

"Us men should be thankful for small mercies," Dave told me. "Are you thankful enough?"

"I am, boss, I sure am," I said humbly.

Rachel ignored this exchange. "I know what we can do," she said slowly.

"Drag Gleeson into the boiler room, tie him to the pipes, blindfold him and spout politically-correct feminism at him, day and night for a month, until he sees the error of his ways?" Dave suggested.

"You've been watching too many spy films," I said.

Rachel brushed off Dave's sarcasm. "No, better than that. Start a newspaper!"

"A newspaper?" Dave and I repeated together. We sounded like Lady Bracknell enquiring about handbags.

"That's a great idea, Rache." Marie-Claire caught the suggestion and ran with it. "Monkscross ought to have a school newspaper – if other schools can do it, why can't we? We could have all sorts of things in it, short stories, poems . . ."

"Cookery, fashion, how to prepare cooked salmon on a primus stove in your back garden while wearing this season's shortest-of-short shorts and a bikini top . . ." Dave interrupted.

"That's the Boy Scouts's manual," I pointed out.

"It's sexist, that's what it is," Rachel said. "And that's what *our* paper's going to campaign against. If Franklin won't act, we will. The pen is mightier than the sword. Look at Watergate."

"Do we have to?" Dave asked. "Nixon never turned me on."

"What about the libel laws?" I asked.

Rachel bit her lip. "Mmm. You're right, that might be a problem. Not that anyone would bother to sue us, but they'd shut us down immediately we got close to the bone."

"You could always run a *samizdat*."

"A what?" Dave asked. "Isn't that what Russians drink tea from?"

"No, that's a samovar. Get your Russian right. A *samizdat*'s a secret underground paper. Like the Soviet dissidents published before the fall of Communism."

"Communism had a lot going for it," Rachel said.

"Oh, God," Dave groaned. "So now we have a militant feminist *communist* newspaper. Good night."

"We'd have to put in other things too," Rachel said. "Appeal to a wide readership."

"You mean someone else besides yourself?"

"Will you be serious? I think we could do a really good paper. Marie-Claire could be literary editor and ask for stories and poems. Hugh could do computers and films, you could be in charge of the music page – you're into that, and we'd all do topical political articles, which would be the main thing, only people won't realise that, if we're clever, and buy it for all the rest."

"Hmm." She'd got at Dave where he was most vulnerable. "It would be interesting to write about the music scene. Educate the dweebs into what music *should* be. But not if it's going to be a feminist rag. I have my principles."

"OK. We do articles on rights for everyone. Ask people to write in about what really bugs them."

"Even scum like Gleeson complaining about being bugged by people like you?"

Rachel shrugged. "I suppose so. Either speech is free or it isn't. But *we* have editorial control."

"I thought you said either speech was free or it wasn't."

"It is. Anyone can say anything they like. But we will also have a chance to put *our* point of view."

"So we're back to getting at Gleeson again?"

Rachel grinned. "Maybe. But there are more ways than one of skinning a cat."

"Taxidermy as well?" I raised my eyebrows. "This is going to be some newspaper, folks."

"Are you in?" Rachel asked me directly.

"Me? In? How could I be otherwise? Would I miss the publishing event of the year?"

"OK, then. We'd better get moving. I suppose I'd better ask Franklin for permission."

"Are you sure you want to see Frankenstein again so soon?" Dave asked. "Don't you think you should lie low for a while?"

"He'll approve of this: it shows initiative and creativity. I'll see him tomorrow, and then we can put up a notice asking for contributions. All of you think of a title," she said, as her bus squealed to a halt at the stop.

"Rachel's Rant?" Dave suggested, once she was safely out of earshot. *"The Rabid Raver?"*

"I think it's a good idea, anyway," Marie-Claire said firmly.

And at that stage, I agreed with her.

Chapter 6

> Paper was invented in China about 105 AD, by Ts'ai Lun, a eunuch - the only eunuch of importance in the history of technology.

"OK," Rachel told us in the canteen the next day. "I've checked with the Head and the paper has his official blessing."

"How nice," Dave said.

"He thinks it's an excellent idea," she went on, "as long as I remember it's a school newspaper we're hoping to produce and not a propaganda sheet." She grinned. "He says he's sure he can trust us to reflect the ethos of the school. Now why should he think we'd want to do anything else?"

"Why indeed?" I echoed. "I'm sure nothing was further from your mind."

"What would you say was the ethos of the school?" Dave asked. "Don't cause any trouble?"

"Keep to the left side of the corridors," I suggested.

"You know what he means," Marie-Claire interrupted. "Sort of liberal, thinking of others, all that."

Rachel ignored us. "I've also seen Ms Blenchley and she said we can use the school computers and the photocopier. But we have to provide our own paper, which might be expensive."

"D'you think?" Dave's voice was suspiciously innocent. "I mean, what sort of readership are you aiming at? There'll be the four of us, of course, and then our 'doting mums and grannies', to quote Creepy Chris, and maybe one or two fellow pupils whose arms we can twist . . . I'd say you should manage with about one A4 pad."

"Listen. This is going to be a serious paper. It's going to be *good.* If all you can do is make stupid jokes about it, then forget it."

"We could put in advertisements," Marie-Claire suggested. "Maybe local shops would pay to have an ad in?"

"Ah, but that would mean entering the muddy waters of capitalism," Dave said. "I thought we were going to stay pure."

If Rachel's look had been loaded, Dave would have been blown away.

"OK," I asked her, "how many copies are we going to try to print? Are we hoping to sell it to most of the school? If so, we'll need what? Eight, nine hundred copies?"

Dave raised an eyebrow. "Eight or nine hundred? Get real! What do you think we're talking about here, the *Sun*? Mind you," he added, "if you *really* want to sell to most of the school, that might be an idea. A page-three pin-up with every copy! Alternate bimbos and Chippendales to cater for both sexes and keep Rachel happy!"

"I don't think we should be too ambitious to start off with," Marie-Claire said quickly. "Say fifty or a hundred. We could probably raise the money ourselves for that. We'd get it back from the sales."

"Always assuming there are any." I turned to Rachel.

"How often are you hoping to bring out this thing? Every day? Every week?"

"Every year?" Dave suggested.

"I was thinking maybe once a week. We can see how it goes."

"There's no harm in looking for sponsorship," I said.

"You're right," Rachel agreed. "We probably will have expenses: apart from the actual paper, there'll be things like bus fares to interview people and whatever. And we mightn't sell all the copies we print, especially the first issue. We may have to build up a readership gradually." She turned to me: "Who do you think would lend us money?"

"'Neither borrower nor a lender be'," Dave quoted solemnly. "Shakespeare. *Hamlet.*"

"My, we are intellectual today, aren't we?" I mocked. "Anyway, who's talking of borrowing?"

"Rachel was," Dave said.

I turned to Rachel. "I say that one of us goes round the local shops and tries our luck."

"Would you do it?" she asked.

"OK. I don't mind." The idea of running a newspaper appealed to me: it was better than trying to start a second-rate band any day.

Dave grinned. "I always fancied you as an entrepreneur, mate, your belly supported by a massive desk, a blonde with a shorthand pad perched on the corner of it, waiting to take down your every word."

"You mean I get my very own bimbo? Great."

Rachel sighed.

Marie-Claire smiled.

"Has anyone come up with a name for it yet?" Dave asked as the bell rang for the end of lunch break. "You didn't much go for my suggestions yesterday."

"What about *The Monkscross Monitor*?" That was Marie-Claire.

"Nah. Too naff."

"News of the School? The Daily Scholar? The As-Independent-As-They'll-Allow-Us-To-Be?" I put in.

"No," said Rachel. *"The Door"*.

I raised an eyebrow. "As in, Ms Blenchley-stroke-Frankenstein showed us the door?"

"No, as in Miroslav Holub."

"Jesus, here we go again," Dave groaned. *"Who?"*

"Holub. The Czech poet we did in English last year."

"We did *poetry* last year?" Dave looked amazed.

"Last year," Rachel said slowly and clearly, "when you two dumbheads were in the same class as Marie-Claire and myself for English, we studied modern poetry. Including Miroslav Holub. Right?"

"Ignore them," Marie-Claire told her. "I think that's a great idea. *'Go out and open the door . . .'* That was it, wasn't it. How did it end? *'At least there'll be a draught.'*"

Rachel nodded. "That's what we want to create. A draught in this establishment. Let in a bit of fresh air."

"I hope you've got your scarf and your woolly hat ready," Dave said to me as we went off to our next class. "If Rachel has her way on this, we might find ourselves caught less in a draught than in a hurricane. You know the sort of articles she's likely to write. Is it worth facing possible expulsion just to get in with our Rache?"

Getting in with Rachel was the last thing on my mind. At that stage, my enthusiasm for her newspaper was just that: enthusiasm for her newspaper. Although I admired her intellect, I wasn't sure that I even *liked* her as a person: she reminded me too much of a black widow spider. And not just because she was short and round and tended to wear black all the time.

(For those of you who don't watch nature programmes, the female black widow spider is an even greater feminist than Rache: she eats her husband alive once he's fulfilled his purpose. I've seen it on the telly and, take my word for it, it's not a pretty sight.)

Chapter 7

coffee, asking a woman student out for. Professor Alan Charles Kors of the University of Pennsylvania warns that a male faculty menber who asks female students "out for coffee or a drink to talk about Wittgenstein, God, death, or, for that matter, liberty," is leaving himself open to accusations of sexual harassment or worse.

coffee, failing to ask a woman student out for. The Barnard/Columbia Women's Handbook warns that a male faculty member who "shuns female students outside of class . . . for fear of accusation of sexual harassment," is guilty of a subtle but harmful form of sexism that can seriously "impact our performance in the classroom and our plans for future study."

Sex and Dating, The Official Politically Correct Guide,
Beard & Cerf, HarperCollins

We were sitting at lunch the following Saturday, Ma, Dad and myself, all tucking into home-made soup and pâté, when the phone rang.

"Leave it," Ma ordered. "We're eating."

"But it might be important!" I squealed, pushing back my chair.

"If it is, they'll ring again. Sit down."

"But . . ."

The phone went dead.

I sat down and glared at her.

Dad winked. "Don't worry, son. If she's serious, she'll ring back."

Why do parents have this hang-up about sex? If you *don't* have a girlfriend, they keep making suggestive remarks like that. If you *do*, they're never off your case.

"It could have been for you," I told him. "Maybe it was Madonna deciding she's into balding middle-aged men. Or the Lotto to tell Ma she's won two million pounds. And now we'll never know what you've both missed."

The phone rang again, half an hour later. It was Dave. "I figured you weren't allowed to leave the table. I keep forgetting your Ma has this not-at-meals, not-after-ten-at-night thing. Listen: it's a great day. Why don't we ask the girls to come to Enniskerry or somewhere with us? What d'you think?"

I looked out of the window: spring had arrived – or was passing through fleetingly on its way to somewhere else. The sun was doing its thing out of a cloudless blue sky, the birds were going mad in the bushes, the daffodils, primulas, tulips and wallflowers were all a credit to Ma in the back garden and the sap was rising everywhere, not least in me.

"OK," I said.

"You ring Rachel. I'll ask Marie-Claire."

So that was it. Dave really *was* interested in Marie-Claire. Rachel and I were obviously being asked along to give him a bit of protective cover, but I wasn't proud – an afternoon in the country was better than anything the parents might have lined up for me. I found Rachel's number in the phone book: at least I knew her address now, after seeing her home the weekend before.

A small child answered the phone. "Hello!"

"Hello. Can I speak to Rachel, please?"

"Wha. . . ?"

"Rachel. Can I speak to Rachel?"

There was a crash that almost shattered my eardrum. Then, "I had it first!" "Gimme it!" "It's mine!"

Finally one of the junior voices went "Hello?" again.

Had I got the wrong number? Rachel had never mentioned she had younger siblings. Come to think of it, Rachel never spoke about her family at all. I realised that what I knew about her private life would fit on the back of a 32p stamp.

"Rachel," I repeated patiently. "I'm looking for Rachel Cross. Is she there? Will one of you please go and get her?" I began to get an idea of what infant-school teachers have to put up with. They definitely deserve a rise.

"What are you two doing?" a female voice, full of suspicion, yelled in the distance. "God! Is someone on the phone? If that's Pete, I'll murder the two of you!"

Steps thudded on the stairs.

"Are you Pete?" once of the junior voices asked.

There was another tussle at the far end of the phone. I held the receiver away from my ear.

"Hello? Pete?" The voice was eager, and too young to be Rachel's ma. Did Rachel have a boyfriend? She couldn't have. Not Rachel.

"I'm sorry about that," the voice gabbled on. "It's the twins, they're impossible sometimes. I'll swing for them one day. Pete? *Pete?*"

"It's Hugh," I said.

"Hugh?" The voice went flat. "Hugh what?"

"Hugh O'Connor." Excellent for the ego, this.

"Do I know you?"

Even more flattering. "I thought you did. School, remember?"

"School? Oh, it's Rachel you want. *Rache!*"

"What?" Another female voice. Again from a distance.

"It's some boy for you. On the phone."

"Rachel's got a boyfriend! Rachel's got a boyfriend!" sang the junior chorus.

"Shut up, you two! Hurry up, Rache." Then, to me, "She's just coming. Only don't be long: other people need to use this phone."

A short silence. Had she hung up on me? Then Rachel's voice, nearer this time: "Who is it?"

"I dunno. But whoever it is, will you just try to keep it short – I'm expecting a call from Pete."

"Hello?"

"Hi," I said warily. "Is that you, Rache? It's Hugh here."

"Hugh? Oh."

OK, I didn't expect her to throw her arms, metaphorically speaking, round my neck, but it wouldn't have hurt her to be a bit more enthusiastic. "That's right, Hugh. I realize I'm neither Pete nor Prince Charming, but I do my best."

"Sorry. I was in the kitchen. What do you want?"

I could have put the phone down then. I didn't though. "Me and Dave were wondering if you and Marie-Claire would like to come out this afternoon. Go to the country somewhere. What do you think?"

She didn't answer.

"It's such a lovely day," I ploughed on. "It'd be a shame to waste it." I sounded just like Ma.

"It *is* a beautiful day," she said. There was another minute's silence. Then, "Wait a minute."

She must have put her hand over the phone because I could only hear muffled voices. There seemed to be another argument going on.

Her hand slipped and the phone came alive again. ". . . and

if you think I'm going to tie myself up when Pete might want to take me out, you need your head examined!"

"It's my Saturday off."

"Yeah, I know. But you said you'd swap with me; you can't change now. And I'll make it up to you. Only not today! Give us a break, Rache! You know how long I've fancied Pete. And we really got on last night. I just know he's going to ring today and when he does, I have to be ready."

"You don't *have* to be anything." Ah, Rachel, the incorrigible feminist we knew and loved. Well, whatever. "He can come round here, if he wants to see you."

"So can your fellow. Or we can both go out. Well, we *can*. Dad's upstairs, after all."

I heard Rachel sigh. "Yeah. Sure." Then she spoke directly into the phone again: "Sorry, Hugh. Not today. But thanks for asking."

"Ah, come on, Rache. It'll be good."

"Sorry. See you on Monday. Enjoy yourselves."

This time the phone really did go dead.

I thought of inviting one of my harem of possible girlfriends to come out with us, but who was I kidding? So I rang Dave to call the whole thing off.

Plans had changed. Marie-Claire, in her usual generous fashion, had phoned Stuart Kinsella and some of the others from the play, and rent-a-crowd was on its way. So what could I do but go along too?

We cycled out into the country, a whole load of us, and had a great time. We did all sorts of childish things, damming the stream, climbing the rocks, swinging out of trees. Various people paired off and disappeared for a while, including Dave and Marie-Claire.

It was a pity Rachel missed all the fun.

Chapter 8

The first known political cartoon was printed in 1747 in a pamphlet called *Plain Truth*, published by Benjamin Franklin.

When Marie-Claire invited me to join herself and Dave at a gig the following night, I declined: the two of them were becoming an item, and gooseberries were not my favourite fruit. It wasn't that I minded that Dave had found himself a girlfriend. Not really. But Dave and I had been messing around together since we first met up under the nature table in Miss Leverett's infant class: if he was going to be taken out of circulation, I would either have to find a new best mate or get a woman myself. What I needed, I told myself, was a gorgeous female with a sense of humour who would adore the ground I walked upon. Not easy in these modern times, but surely not impossible either.

I went into school the next Monday with a mission: get myself a girlfriend and start partying.

The first thing I saw was a notice on the Transition Year board. A very large, eye-catching notice done in the sort of psychedelic colours you don't really need first thing on a Monday morning.

Want to achieve fame and immortality?
GET INTO JOURNALISM!
Air your OPINION
Have your poem/cartoon/short story PUBLISHED!
Come to room C2 at 4 pm today
and
FIND OUT MORE!

Oh dear. I had almost forgotten Rachel's newspaper. And it would be *Rachel*'s newspaper, that was for sure. Although I quite fancied myself as a journalist, you didn't need to be psychic to guess that working with Rachel as an editor might be something less than a laugh a minute.

I expected her to twist our arms about the 4 pm meeting when we met up in the canteen over lunch, but she didn't show.

"Where's Rache?" I asked Marie-Claire.

"She said she had to do something."

Dave reached across to grab the salt and poured it over his chips. We'd just come from Biology and a lesson on how too much salt hardens your arteries (which, in case you haven't got that far in the textbook, leads to heart attacks and strokes); either Dave hadn't been listening or he didn't care. "Did you see her notice?"

"Difficult not to," I told him.

"Are you going along?"

"Dunno. Are you?"

"We'd better all go," Marie-Claire said. "To give her support."

"Show solidarity?" Dave kept his face straight.

"Stand by your man," I added my bit.

"Or woman," Dave said. "Though sometimes it's hard to tell the difference."

Marie-Claire looked at us suspiciously. "Rachel's not as

strong as people think she is, you know. She needs friends just like everyone else."

"Yeah. So did Dracula."

"If she needs friends, she has a funny way of showing it," I said, remembering the phone call on Saturday morning.

Marie-Claire nodded her head solemnly, looking like one of the three wise monkeys. "It's strange, isn't it? Rachel's always been popular enough. But you're right, Hugh, she doesn't seem to have real friends. Not the way other people do. I mean, I've been in the same class as her for almost four years, but this is the first year I've become friendly with her. And that's only because of the play. The party the other weekend was the first party I've ever seen her at."

"Theme for this week's Life Skills assignment," Dave mocked. "*Does Rachel Cross have a life?* Apart from women's lib committee meetings, that is?"

"Will you put a sock in it?"

Dave removed one of his runners, took off his sock and dangled it over Marie-Claire's plate of salad. "For you, anything," he said.

Gleeson came past and leered down at us. "Having fun, David?" he asked. "Are you trying to draw attention to yourself (and, if so, are you waving or drowning: read Stevie Smith's poem, if you don't catch the allusion)? Or is this just a statement about school dinners?"

Dave put his sock back on. "Sleazebag," he muttered as Gleeson moved out of earshot. "One day, that guy's going to get what's coming to him."

"Yeah," I agreed, "and one day pigs'll fly."

We went to the meeting at 4 pm. There was obviously not a lot of interest in fame and immortality in Monkscross Comprehensive: apart from ourselves, five people turned up. I was glad we'd given in to Marie-Claire and come along.

They were keen, though, the five others. Brian was into

crosswords and jokes. I knew his sense of humour, having sat beside him through Life Skills last term and put up with his wit, but I supposed that we had to appeal to all tastes.

Kerry offered to do fashion. She was a friend of Marie-Claire's.

Louise was in the same form as Dave and myself: she played hockey, golf and tennis, *and* swam for the Leinster Province Under-Sixteen team; her big ambition was to take over the sports department at RTE and she must have felt that any sort of sports journalism, even working on a school newspaper, would be a start. It didn't bother me: if we wanted decent sales, we had to keep the sporting types with us.

Kate, a new girl who had only joined the school at Christmas, was into art. I hardly knew her, but Dave had tried to get off with her on some trip or other and didn't like her. He thought she was arrogant. But then, of course, having been turned down by her he would, wouldn't he?

And the last was a weedy lad from first year, called Finn, who thought we were auditioning for the school orchestra but who stayed on even after he'd discovered his mistake because he'd told his Mummy he'd be late and she wasn't coming to pick him up until 4.30.

Kate wanted to draw cartoons. Political cartoons. "Like *Doonesbury*," she said.

The others looked blank.

"Don't any of you read *The Irish Times*?" Rachel asked.

They looked even blanker.

"It's a great idea," Rachel told her. "I was hoping the paper would be politically conscious and a regular cartoon would certainly help. But if this lot's a representative sample of our readership, don't expect anyone to understand what you're doing." She turned on the rest of us: "How many political parties can you name and who leads them?"

"What's this?" Brian asked, sulking. "Some sort of a test?"

"Just answer the question. How many political parties and their leaders can you name?"

"Haughey."

"No, you idiot," said Kerry. "He's gone."

"Fianna Fáil, Fine Gael, Labour, Progressive Democrats, Workers' Party, Greens." That was Finn. He sounded as bored as he looked.

"Who are the party leaders, then?" Rachel insisted.

"Mary Robinson."

"De Valera."

"Brian Boru."

"Zig and Zag."

"Donald Duck."

Rachel looked at Kate. "See what I mean?"

"OK, then. I'll build it round school politics."

I remembered a television programme I'd seen once on body language: Rachel's body language was that of a tiger who has just sighted an antelope at a waterhole.

"You don't have Creepy Chris for English, do you?" she asked Kate.

"Creepy who?"

"Mr Gleeson."

"Is that what you call him? Creepy Chris?"

"When she can't think of anything worse," Dave said darkly.

"Mmm. That sort of makes sense. He does give you the creeps."

"Could you do a cartoon around *him*?"

"You mean you can get away with something like that in this school?"

"You can't," Marie-Claire said. "We'd be shut down on the very first issue. Attacking teachers is just not on."

Rachel smiled. If I had been Gleeson, I wouldn't have liked that smile. "I wasn't suggesting we name him outright. I'm not as thick as that. But we could run a cartoon about sexual harassment . . ."

"Here we go, here we go, here we go again," Dave sang under his breath.

". . . without naming him. People would know who we were talking about. The beauty of it is that he wouldn't be able to defend himself without agreeing that it was *him* the cartoon was about, so we would get away with it."

"Is this paper going to be all feminist stuff?" Brian asked in disgust. "If it is, I'm out of here."

"Nah," I said quickly, before Rachel could call out a lynch mob. "Definitely hermaphrodite."

"Definitely what?" Kerry asked.

"Jocks as well as bimbos, he means," Dave interpreted. "In your fashion articles," he added when she looked even more confused.

Marie-Claire intervened, tactful as ever. "Is it OK if I put up a notice on the main notice-board asking for stories and poems? Or should we keep it to Transition Year only?"

"As it's a Transition Year paper, maybe we should keep it to the year," Kate said. "What does everyone else think?"

"If we're going to try to flog it to the whole school, we'd better let the whole school have a piece of it," I suggested.

"OK," Rachel said. "We'll put up a notice asking for any contributions from the public. We could do a letters page, for a start."

"What about a problem page?" Dave suggested. *"Dear Auntie Mabel. My boyfriend doesn't love me because my clothes aren't washed in White-Oh. What shall I do?"* He appealed to Rachel: "Please, Miss, can I write that?"

I looked at my watch. Time was marching on and Tom and

Jerry were waiting for me at home. "OK, people. Let's decide what we're doing and get out of here. At the moment we have," I ticked them off on my fingers, "a sports page, Louise; a fashion page, Kerry; a music page, Dave; crosswords and jokes, Brian; computer and films, not to mention PR man, me; literary page, Marie-Claire; graphic art, Kate; and rampant feminism plus political correctness, Rachel." I smiled sweetly at her.

"Drop dead," she suggested.

"So why don't you all go off now and do your own things. All contributions to be in by . . . when, Rache?"

"Say next Monday at the latest? That'll give everyone the weekend."

"OK. All contributions to be in by this day week. We'll have another meeting then, same time, same place. Any questions?"

"No, *mein Führer.*" Dave gave me a fascist salute.

"And up yours too, mate."

Maybe I'm cut out for the big bad world of management after all, I thought on the bus home. Prop up a desk with my belly, as Dave had suggested, for the next forty years? Ma *would* be pleased!

Chapter 9

During their lifetime, the average person spends
7 years in the bathroom
6 years eating
5 years standing in queues
4 years doing household chores
2 years trying to return phone calls to people who are unavailable
1 year searching for lost objects
8 months opening junk mail
6 months waiting at traffic lights
2.5 months at the cinema

The week passed uneventfully. I sussed out a few of the local shops and managed to persuade two of them to come up with £25 each to sponsor an ad in the paper. I was quite pleased with myself: £50 would easily cover our expenses for the first issue.

Apart from that, we went to school, messed about, listened to some music (Dave was taking his job as a music critic seriously), took in a film (for the sake of my column) and a jazz session (for the sake of Dave's), negotiated with the parents over the usual issues (tidiness, homework, housework, tidiness, curfews, tidiness – as I said, the usual) ate, watched TV and slept. Which didn't leave much time for item number two on my agenda: finding myself a nice old-fashioned girl to be loved by.

On Saturday morning, Dave and I bumped into Marie-Claire outside *Virgin Megastore* on Aston Quay. We took her to the *Winding Stair Bookshop* for coffee. Marie-Claire had never been there, of course. She found it 'interesting'.

"Do either of you believe this newspaper's actually going to work?" Dave asked as we sat round a table. "I mean, writing articles for it's worse than homework: I don't know why you all took the piss out of my idea of starting a band."

"It'll be fine. Rachel will see to that. She's a woman determined to change the world, our Rache."

"I worry about her," Marie-Claire said. "I mean, she never seems to *do* anything. It's much more obvious since we were all in the play together that she's got absolutely no social life . . ."

"Oh dearie me!" Dave looked horrified. "Absolutely no social life! How dreadful!"

Marie-Claire glared at him. "You know what I mean. She's always rushing off home. She never seems to go out anywhere."

"Yeah," I said, remembering how she'd been so anxious to get home from the party after the final night of the play. I grinned. "Maybe she turns into a werewolf at midnight?"

"You'd better watch it if she does, mate." Dave raised his nose into the air and let out a howl, causing a sudden silence in the coffee shop, followed by nasty looks from most of the customers and a warning scowl from the girl behind the counter. "Get in with her any more and you'll find yourself at the wrong end of the Red Riding Hood story."

"You're not funny, you know that?" I told him.

"She never speaks about her family," Marie-Claire went on, like a dog worrying a bone. "Or about herself at all. I've *never* heard her talk about her private life. It's not normal."

"Not for a girl, anyway," Dave said.

Marie-Claire pretended not to hear him. "You don't think she's . . . there's something wrong . . . at home, do you? You know all these reports about, well, incest and stuff you read in the papers. The victims never talked about what was going on. Maybe that's what's happening to Rachel?"

Dave laughed. "I pity anyone who tried to have it off with Rachel. I doubt if they'd survive with their manhood intact."

At the rate he was going, Dave's own survival rate was equally at risk. "Give it a rest, Marie-Claire," I said soothingly. "You've always had an overactive imagination – it probably goes with the literary skills. Stop worrying. She's OK."

"I don't know." Marie-Claire wouldn't let herself be cheered up. "I asked her to come into town with me today and she refused. She said she had things to do."

"Maybe she has," Dave said. "My parents expected me to do things today too. That's what parents believe weekends are for. Luckily, I got out just in time."

I backed him up in changing the subject. "You think you've got problems? My dad wanted me to go jogging this morning. Jogging! He's known me for fifteen years now, and he still thinks I might like to join him trotting round the neighbourhood in a pair of boxer shorts."

Dave grinned. "Perhaps he thinks you need the exercise."

"Nah. You know the Oldies: if you're still in bed at ten in the morning, it drives them out of their skulls. I mean, according to Dad, the only chance you got to have a lie-in when *he* was young was if you had a temperature of a hundred and ten and were on your deathbed; and that only if your parents were feeling soft that day. They've told themselves that crap so often they actually believe it themselves now."

"D'you think Rachel might come to a film with us if we all went together?" Marie-Claire asked. "She needs to get out. It's not healthy being on your own all the time."

"I asked her to come with us last weekend, remember. And she wasn't interested."

"I'd hate to give you a complex, mate, but it might just possibly be you. Did you brush your teeth with the right toothpaste and put on the right deodorant? Did you?"

"I was on the phone, remember?"

"Amazing what can travel down a phone line these days."

"Yeah. Sure." I turned to Marie-Claire. "OK, ask her. I suppose I ought to see another film this week if I'm going to write a decent column."

"How much did you say you got in sponsorship?" Dave asked. "Can we use it for expenses?"

Dave was right: all these cultural outings were mounting up.

I backtracked. "Or we could get out a couple of videos and watch them at my place. Then I'd have a film and two videos to write about and it wouldn't cost an arm and three legs."

"Is there anything in the video shop that would be highbrow enough for our Rachel?" Dave asked.

He was beginning to annoy me. "What have you got against her? She's not that bad."

"No?"

I turned my back on him. "That's fixed then, Marie-Claire. Come round to my place tomorrow night. Bring Rachel and a bowl of popcorn."

"In any order." Dave couldn't resist having the last word.

Rachel turned us down. I began to wonder if Marie-Claire's suspicions were correct about her home life. Was there some evil lurking behind the middle-class curtains of the Cross ménage?

Nah, I thought, the Oldies are right: TV rots your mind and gives you weird ideas. If I didn't watch out, I'd turn into as much of a worrier as Marie-Claire.

Chapter 10

> Women constitute half of the world's population, perform nearly two-thirds of its work hours, receive one fourth of the world's income, and own less than one hundredth of the world's property.

The first meeting of the newspaper staff took place after school on Monday. Amazingly, everyone had actually put in some work and met the deadline. It must be the novelty, I thought. Give it a week or two . . .

Brian handed in two crosswords and a page full of jokes, Louise an in-depth report on the under-14s hockey match plus the result of every match played by every team in the school the previous week (she would obviously have included the tiddlywinks club, too – if we'd had a tiddlywinks club), Kerry's half-page on fashions looked OK, Marie-Claire had produced a short story of her own and a couple of book reviews, Dave had written a long article on the current music scene in Dublin and I'd managed to come up with one film review, one video review and a computer column. I don't know about anyone else, but I'd been up till well after midnight the night before, trying to get my stuff finished: if anyone tells you journalism is easy, don't buy a used car from them.

The only person who had answered our appeal for contributions was a lad called Jonathan. He had left in some of his poems. Twenty-three of his poems, to be exact.

"OK," Rachel said crisply. "So nobody else in the school wants to help. I'm not surprised – the apathy in this place is mind-blowing. We'll do the first issue ourselves."

"You're forgetting Monkscross's answer to Seamus Heaney," I pointed out.

She didn't find this funny. "Just pick a couple of his shorter ones, Marie-Claire."

"What about my *Dear Auntie Mabel* column?" Dave wanted to know.

"I thought you were doing music?" Brian said.

"I'm ambidextrous. I can do both."

Brian looked confused.

Rachel grinned. "OK then, go ahead. But be sensible. Don't mess around."

"Would I?" Dave asked innocently.

"I'll fake a few letters for the letters page," Rachel went on, "just to get the ball rolling. With any luck one of them will start a controversy and people will want to reply."

I couldn't help wondering which would be the most outrageous: Dave's imaginary *Dear Auntie Mabel* column or Rachel's imaginary letters. It would be a close thing.

Rachel cleared her throat. "The first edition is going to be terribly important. If we get it right, people will want to buy *The Door* again. If it's wrong, we might as well give up." She took a piece of paper from her folder. "I've done an editorial. I think it works, but we'll just have to wait and see."

Dave grabbed it from her. "Hi, Monkscrossites!" he read out loud to the rest of us.

"This is the first issue of our new Transition Year Newspaper, *The Door*. But you don't have to be in Transition Year to read it. And we hope any of you out there with something to say will write in. We want to hear from you. All of you. No matter what your views are.

"Because this is going to be a crusading newspaper. The pen is mightier than the sword and journalism CAN change the world. Believe it.

"We want, as our title implies, to open a door. To quote Miroslav Holub:

Go out and open the door.
    Maybe outside there's
    a tree or a wood,
    a garden,
    or a magic city.

Go and open the door.
    Maybe a dog's rummaging.
    Maybe you'll see faces,
or an eye,
or the picture
            of a picture.

Go and open the door.
    If there's a fog
    it will clear.

Go and open the door.
    Even if there's only
    the darkness ticking,
    even if there's only
    the hollow wind,

even if
nothing
is there,
go and open the door.

At least
there'll be
a draught.

"Help us to make a draught in this school! Read *The Door* and write in about anything you really care about!"

There was a silence. If Brian had looked confused before, he looked positively stunned now. Kerry was smiling brightly, but I doubt if she had much of a clue either.

"Strong stuff," Dave said, suspiciously mildly, as he put down the piece of paper.

"Er. Um. Are you sure quoting the whole poem is a good idea?" I asked. Mr Tactful, that's me.

"Yes," Rachel said.

I decided not to argue with her.

"I think it's great," said Marie-Claire.

Kate looked thoughtful, but didn't comment.

"All that about the pen being mightier than the sword and journalism changing the world – isn't it a bit over the top?" Louise asked.

"No," Rachel said.

'Never apologise, never explain,' that's what they advise, isn't it? Rachel had it down to a fine art.

It worked, too. We forgot about her editorial and started discussing how soon we could get the paper out. We decided that, if Louise's sports news and my stuff about films wasn't going to be *totally* out of date, it had to come out that week.

Which meant having it finished on Wednesday and on sale by Thursday, to give us a bit of time in case something went wrong somewhere. Rachel offered (offered?!) to take everyone else's articles home with her and edit them.

"OK, so," she said. "Everybody come to the computer room after school tomorrow. I'll work out the column width and we'll put everything into the computers and print it out. I'll do the layout tomorrow night and then some of us can meet again on Wednesday to photocopy the finished sheets."

"You're joking," Dave groaned. "This is worse than detention."

"I've got training tomorrow," Louise said. "I won't be able to help."

"OK, we don't all have to do the typing. Just as long as we get it done. Kate's going to work on the illustrations as soon as she sees your articles, so they'll be ready tomorrow too."

Which reminded me. "How's the cartoon coming along?" I asked.

"We're getting there," Kate said. Enigmatically, I think is the right word. Sort of Mona-Lisa-ish, anyway.

"Who's we?" I asked, a nasty suspicion dawning on me. If Rachel was helping Kate with this anti-Gleeson cartoon, anything could happen.

My guess was right: "We're doing it together", Rachel said. She started to gather up her things. "That's about it. The only thing left to decide is the logo and Kate's offered to come up with a couple of designs. We can decide which one we like best tomorrow."

"We?" Dave asked. "Is that the royal 'we' or do the rest of us also have a say in this?"

"Of course you do. Everyone has a say. This is going to be a democratic newspaper."

Nobody challenged her. We all handed over our

masterpieces, like good little schoolchildren, and trooped out of the room.

"All power corrupts, absolute power corrupts absolutely," Dave quoted as we walked together down to the bus, the girls having stayed behind to discuss illustrations with Kate. "I hate bossy women."

"It's not so much Rachel's bossiness that worries me, it's what she might be getting up to," I said thoughtfully. "Maybe it's not such a good idea to let her loose on the paper, all on her own."

"If she wants to do most of the work, that's OK by me."

"No. I mean, just think about it: Rachel with a whole newspaper to get at everyone she disapproves of. And there's that cartoon she and Kate are doing, the one that's meant to be out to get Gleeson. We could be in real trouble over that."

"So what are you going to do about it? Censor her stuff? Just make sure you leave me any of your decent tapes and let us know whether you want to be buried or cremated."

I had got myself seriously worried now. "Listen," I told him, "she's capable of printing *anything*. We've got to find out what she means to put in. We'll have to insist on seeing *everything* before anyone starts typing their stuff into the computers tomorrow."

Dave kicked a stone along the pavement. "When? At lunch break? This newspaper is playing hell with my digestion already."

"It's either that or adding our names to something we know nothing about. Rachel is ruthless when it comes to a cause. And Kate seems to be as bad. I don't trust either of them."

"Me neither. But is it worth the hassle of starting a fight with them?"

"Aw, come on, Dave. Are you with me or not?"

"Why not let them go ahead and print whatever they want? I mean, if we know what's going to be in, we'll have to do something about it. If we don't know, nobody can blame us for anything they write. It makes sense to me."

"I'm going to insist on seeing it anyway."

"You intending to take a course before tomorrow?"

"A course?"

"Yeah. In assertiveness training."

"Come off it, Dave. Rachel can't do anything to us."

"I wouldn't bet on it. However, for old time's sake . . ." Dave put down his bag and pulled out his ruler. Holding it out towards me, he pledged: "All for one and one for all!"

I found my ruler and did likewise.

An old lady walked her dog round us, tut-tutting as she went.

Chapter 11

> Quite a number of his actions and attitudes had in the past struck him as unworthy . . . but doing the necessary things about it was hard. Hard not because he didn't want to change, but because keeping on the alert for being mature and responsible and so on took it out of him.
>
> Kingsley Amis, *I Like it Here.*

So much for solidarity: Dave didn't even show for the meeting the next day. Nor, for that matter, did Brian and Louise.

Rachel handed the rest of us our articles and distributed the other three's between us. "Have a look through them. If you don't like any of the changes I've made or if you find a mistake I've missed, let me know."

"What about your own stuff, Rache?" I asked. "Do you want one of us to check it for you?" Captain Courageous, that's me.

"Kate's looked over it, but thanks all the same."

I made one more try: "Can we see it?"

"We don't have time. Everyone grab a computer and start typing. This has to be finished today."

I did as I was told.

She'd given me Brian's copy as well as my own. I looked through it. "What's this? Censorship?"

"Sorry?"

"Brian's jokes. You've only left him with four."

"Just read the rest. Are you surprised?"

I read them and chuckled. "They're funny."

"They are sexist and racist and vulgar."

Kerry, Marie-Claire and Kate came and looked over my shoulder. Kerry giggled, Marie-Claire blushed, Kate grinned.

"Do you honestly think Ms Blenchley, let alone Franklin, will allow us to get away with that?" Rachel asked.

I saw her point. "Brian's not going to like it, though."

"We've left him four jokes. And his crossword. He should be grateful."

I worked as quickly as I could so that I could wander over to Rachel's computer and sneak a look at the screen, but she'd finished before me. She already had her own print-outs safely tucked away in a folder; she added mine and Brian's to them and waited for the others.

I tried one last time: "Let's have a look at yours, Rache. While we're waiting."

No apology, no explanation, just, "Nope."

I'd love to know how she does it.

"Do you know anything about corporate responsibility?" I asked Dad during a break in the match on the box that evening.

"Corporate responsibility?"

"Yeah. Say, for example, an editor prints something in a newspaper or a magazine. Are the rest of the staff responsible for what she puts in?"

He tore his eyes from the Guinness ad and looked at me. "Any particular reason for the question?"

"It's for a project I'm doing." 'Keep to the truth wherever possible' is my motto.

"Mmm. *She* puts in, you said? I gather there's a female

editor lurking here somewhere? Are you intending to bring her home to meet your mother and myself, or is it not that type of relationship?"

"You've got a one-track mind," I told him. "I just didn't want to be sexist."

He gave me a shrewd look. "Well, I'm no expert on law but I should imagine that, legally, you'll be in the clear for anything this mysterious editor writes. Whether Mr Franklin will abide by the niceties of the law, or will assume that the rest of you are equally guilty for whatever it is *she* intends to publish, is another matter."

I can't say it cheered me up much.

Next day I got my courage together and tackled Rachel over lunch.

"Any chance of a preview of the paper?" I asked innocently. "I'd love to see how you've done the layout."

"Sorry, I left it in the office. I didn't want to drag it round school with me all day."

"We could go down to the office and look at it now."

"Don't you trust me?"

"It's not that." It was, though. Definitely. "It's just that we're all supposed to be in this together."

"So you *don't* trust me!" Rachel gave me a look which would have turned even the fake cream in the jam bun I'd just eaten sour.

I glared back at her: *High Noon* in the canteen.

Marie-Claire looked embarrassed. Dave just grinned.

Rachel was the first to back down. "OK, then. If you insist. It's your lunch break you're wasting." She led us down to the office.

We bumped into Louise on the way and dragged her along, too. I thought she might be useful as back-up: she seemed a sensible sort of a girl.

One of the secretaries, Mrs French, let us in and allowed Rachel to spread the pasted-up sheets over her table.

"Do you need any help?"

She peered over Rachel's shoulder, trying to catch a glimpse of the paper, but Rachel blocked her view. "No, thank you, Mrs French. We're fine."

Mrs French retreated to the switchboard.

We bent over the paste-ups. Rachel had done a good job. The articles were well spaced, separated by Brian's crossword, his jokes and by hand-drawn illustrations in black ink.

"Did Kate do these?" I asked incredulously. They were amazing: zany cartoons for Brian's jokes, fashion drawings for Kerry's article, a cartoon-footballer on Louise's sports page, and a couple having a snog for Marie-Claire's story (she likes romance, does Marie-Claire). The logo was excellent too: a drawing of the front of the school under the heading *The Door.*

"They're good, aren't they?" Rachel said. "Kate worked on them with me last night."

So Kate had actually been in Rachel's house. Which was more than could be said for the rest of us, even Marie-Claire. I expected Marie-Claire to look narked that the new girl had beaten her to it, but she just seemed delighted that Kate was so talented. "They're *fantastic*," she said, with genuine enthusiasm. Sometimes I wondered if she lived in the same world as the rest of us.

I turned the pages, looking for Rachel and Kate's 'political' cartoon. Halfway down page two there was a column entitled *Ask Mabel.* I glanced at Dave.

He grinned. "Well, we did say we should try and get contributions."

I read the 'letter' he'd written:

Dear Mabel,
I fancy this fellow in my class. He's terrific-looking and a really great guy. He plays the guitar like magic. But I think he's shy. Should I tell him what I feel about him?
Unrequited 4th Year

Dear Unrequited 4th Year,
Go for it!

"Is that it?" I asked.

"You should have seen what his other ones were like," Rachel said darkly. "That was the only half-respectable one."

Dave frowned. "You cut out the most important part of the answer. What I wrote was 'if you're good-looking and the type he'd be interested in, then go for it!' What happened to that bit?"

"Guess," Rachel said.

Page three had her editorial and five "readers' letters". I skimmed the editorial: we'd read it already. Then I looked at the letters. The first one, signed 'Peter', wanted the school to campaign against motorways and for cycle-lanes; the second was signed 'Aoife' and recommended neutering stray cats; the third, signed 'Conor', asked why girls weren't allowed to play rugby; the fourth, by 'Babs', suggested people should join Amnesty International; and the last, by 'June', hoped that the canteen would go vegetarian.

"I didn't know you were into girls' rugby, Rache," I said with, I thought, commendable restraint.

The only other thing she'd done was a piece about waste disposal at Sellafield, which was full of facts and figures and, knowing Rachel, was probably so accurate that not even British Nuclear Fuels could have had us up for libel. And it was a safe enough subject: even Frankenstein could hardly object to us knocking nuclear waste disposal, no matter what his private thoughts on the matter might be.

The cartoon strip was inside the back page. Kate could draw well, I'd seen that already, and it was very professional-looking. It was four frames long.

The first frame showed a romantic, turreted castle set in front of towering snow-capped peaks. The title of the strip was scrawled across the cloudless sky: SWISS VALLEY HIGH. I blinked. The next three frames were even more amazing. "Hi," said a blonde bimbo in a sexy gymslip in the second frame: "I'm Suzie." "And we're Zena, Meredith and Chantelle," pouted the three other bimbos beside her. Although they all had different hairstyles and were of varying shapes and sizes, they had one thing in common: not one of them looked as if she needed self-assertiveness training. No sirree. They looked as if they could eat a wimp each for breakfast and still be hungry. In fact, had they been male, they'd have been hunks with piercing blue eyes and strong manly chins, not to mention broad muscular shoulders: these were no women to mess with.

This, in fact, was the only thing which made sense. I mean, I could see Rachel and Kate writing a strip about super-heroines; what I couldn't understand was why they had set it in a posh girls' finishing school in the Alps. Remember we're talking about Rachel and Kate here, both born-again Marxist feminists. Why, you have to ask yourself, would they set their comic strip (which, don't forget, was supposed to be attacking Gleeson) in an all-girls' boarding school for spoilt rich brats in the most capitalistic country in Europe? It blew the mind.

(The third frame, in case you're interested, had Suzie and company telling you that they all belonged to Year Four at

Swiss Valley School. And in the fourth Suzie stared straight out at you, winked an eye, and promised excitement and thrills in future editions. "So keep watching, friends!")

"It's excellent," Marie-Claire said enthusiastically. "It's really professional."

Louise looked at it again. "Who are you aiming it at? First years?" She grinned. "I somehow didn't see you and Kate being into the *Sweet Valley High* mentality, Rache."

Rachel just smiled.

"I like it," Dave announced. "A bunch of sexy young girls – what more could any man want?"

Amazingly, Rachel's smile broadened. "Good," she said. "I hoped you'd see it that way. So we now have first years and all the males in the school interested. Not bad."

I didn't say anything. I was too amazed. I mean, Rachel going straight for the lowest common denominator! What had happened to her high ideals?

"You should see your face," Rachel told me, looking like a cat who'd just won first prize at Crufts – or whatever show cats win prizes at.

"I won't try to hide the fact that I'm surprised," I said with dignity.

"Good," she said. "We were hoping for that, too."

It's funny: when I thought Rachel and Kate were going to print something about Gleeson that would land us in big trouble, I was all worried. Now that I knew that their famous cartoon was going to be nothing worse than a cross between Enid Blyton and Jilly Cooper, it surprised me to find that I wasn't as relieved as I should have been.

We got the paper photocopied that afternoon and hit the mall with it at lunchtime the next day. Unbelievably, people were actually willing to spend good money on it. We sold over forty copies at 10p a time, which wasn't bad going. It's as well, though, that Brian hadn't made any plans for going to the Bahamas on the profits.

Still, maybe the next edition would do better, once people knew what they were getting. Maybe more people would write in to it, too. And more of them would mean less of Rachel and her causes.

Even the staff were giving us compliments. Frankenstein was delighted: "That's the sort of initiative this year is all about, chil . . . er, young people."

It's a good thing that he wasn't able to see into the future.

Chapter 12

Loan repayments cost poor countries three times more than they receive in official development assistance from abroad.

In terms of consumption of goods, an average North American baby represents twice the damage to the environment of a Swedish baby, 13 times that of a Brazilian, 35 times that of an Indian and 280 times that of a Haitian.

The newspaper became part of our lives. Whatever else was on each week, I had to spend at least one evening checking out the latest film in town and another reviewing a video. It was great to be able to tell the parents this was work, rather than the dossing that they saw it as.

It even crossed my mind to make "film critic" the current answer to that question people have been asking me for as long as I can remember (I wouldn't be surprised if the midwife asked it the moment I plopped on to the delivery table) and which, this year, seems to be the only thing *everyone* is taking seriously: "And what do you want to do when you leave school, Hugh?" Except that I didn't think either Mr Hayward in Careers and Guidance or, especially, Ma and Dad would regard writing film reviews as a proper career. Maybe the oldie generation were programmed from birth to see their whole future in front of them ("I'm gonna' swap this nappy for a pin-striped suit, join a bank and stay there till I'm sixty-five"), but for me, seeing more than the day ahead needs a crystal ball.

Sometimes Dave came with me to the cinema, sometimes Marie-Claire tagged along too, and sometimes there was a whole gang of us. But Rachel never came. Perhaps the films I wanted to see weren't feminist enough for her. Or maybe she had a secret boyfriend and, all the times she fobbed us off, she was meeting him for dark passionate sessions where they'd discuss Marxist-Leninism or how to garrotte fox-hunters. Marie-Claire still worried that there was something wrong at home and suggested, now and again, that we should *do* something about it; but then Marie-Claire would.

Surprisingly, *The Door* was a success, despite Rachel's extremism. The mix was good and I suppose we appealed to all tastes. Louise's sports page was really professional: she had a great future ahead of her as a sports journalist and all the jocks (OK, Rachel, and jockesses) who wouldn't look at a book if it sat up and bit them bought the paper, if only to see if they got a mention. Music, film and computer buffs seemed happy with the stuff Dave and I put in and we'd no shortage of people wanting to write for us. Too many, in fact; the trouble was keeping them away. Kerry's fashion articles were popular too. And contributions had started coming in for Marie-Claire's literary page, some of them really good. There's actually a lot of talent in our school, surprisingly enough.

The letters page in the paper became just that (a letters page rather than an outlet for all Rachel's obsessions) as more and more people wrote in to it. It had sparked off quite a few arguments which was what, she said, she'd been aiming at all along. And Dave even found himself getting real problems sent in to his *Ask Mabel* column. Well, some of them were real; some of them were definite send-ups. (Either that or a lot of people in our school sleep through the sex-education classes.)

Even Brian's jokes, though they'd make you cringe sometimes, had their own fan club, just like the *Swiss Valley High* cartoon.

I read the first few strips, wondering what Kate and Rachel were up to. It was really weird: Rachel, the only fanatical feminist I had ever met, and Kate, who seemed to be pretty much the same way, had put together a cartoon strip which went against all their principles. *Swiss Valley High* was definitely meant to appeal to the masses rather than the intelligentsia: our sexy heroines got up to the usual things girls in Continental boarding-schools get up to, ie have midnight feasts in the dorm, climb out of windows, fall in love with the ski instructor, climb in windows: use your imagination. I was amazed that either Rachel or Kate would churn out such . . . *mush.* Is this what Rachel meant by opening a door?

We still met every Monday to decide what was going to be in the paper, but pretty soon the others were only handing in their copy (and often you'd have a hard time getting that), so that sometimes only Rachel, Marie-Claire and myself turned up. Marie-Claire usually went along with whatever Rachel wanted and so we had articles on women's rights, animal rights, responsible dog ownership, recycling, pollution, racism, nuclear power, bullying . . . you name it, Rachel came up with it. I kept my opposition to things that were really over the top.

What did I learn this year, Ms Blenchley? To be an ombudsman for causes Rachel had it in for.

Chapter 13

After becoming Emperor of Rome, Nero's dearest ambition was to sing in public. Three clever citizens tricked the guards into letting them out of the theatre: one pretended to be dead and the other two carried him out.

Like I said, the school newspaper was doing just fine, but my ambition to find a nice, old-fashioned, worshipping-the-ground-her-man-walks-upon type of girl was getting nowhere. Kerry might have answered, but she was worshipping elsewhere: a jock in fifth year, in fact. And who am I to argue with a six-foot-square hulk in the first fifteen?

It didn't help that Dave and Marie-Claire were becoming an item. More or less, anyway. To an unbiased observer (well, *reasonably* unbiased), it looked like Dave was doing most of the running. I mean, Marie-Claire didn't seem to mind whether she went out with Dave or with both of us. She invited herself and Dave along to see the films I was reviewing and asked me along to the bands Dave was writing about. Maybe she was just taking pity on me but, whatever way you look at it, it didn't add up to the love of the century.

At least, though, Dave had a girl to go out with. I was

stuck with being cheerful, dependable Hugh, everyone's friend but nobody's boyfriend or lover.

You get pissed off with that, I tell you. Apart from the threesomes mentioned above, the main social events in my life seemed to be playing with the cat or going along with Dave to this fellow's garage and joining in a session with what he insisted on calling 'the band'. He hadn't given up: he still thought he could make it in music, form a group that would rule the school, the country, the world.

He'd have to do better than the present set-up, that was for sure. Admittedly, he was a genius on the guitar, but even a genius needs help. Gary, the drummer (and owner of the garage), was strong on volume but found just keeping to the beat an infringement of his personal liberty, while my guitar-playing needs serious work put into it. And life is too short for that. We also lacked a vocalist. Dave, who wrote his own lyrics, fancied himself in the role, but his best friend would have had had to admit that his voice stank. And this best friend told him so.

"If you object to the way I sing, why don't *you* do it?"

"Because, unlike yourself, I *know* I have a voice like a frog with tonsillitis." Ma's phrase that – she doesn't believe in false encouragement. (I sometimes wonder how she ever became a social worker: "OK, Mrs Smith. So you think things are getting better? That you're beginning to cope? Don't kid yourself.")

Dave's mother is quite different from mine, much more laid-back. I never feel in Dave's house that I have to watch where I put my dirty feet or avoid dropping crumbs on the carpet. But even she drew the line at a band in her front room. Me taking my guitar round and the two of us messing about softly (with the emphasis on 'softly') was OK, but drums . . . No way. Which was why we'd ended up in Gary's garage.

What Gary's mother thought of the whole thing I have no

idea. In the half-dozen sessions we had there, I never saw her once.

At that stage, as I've said before, Rachel was just Marie-Claire's friend, or someone we worked with on the school newspaper. I certainly didn't regard *her* as girlfriend material: if I'd wanted a bossy woman running my life, I had Ma.

I suppose my interest in her started a week or so later, when I was coming home from Gary's garage (sounds like a trendy new venue: *Gary's Garage: the grungiest eating place in town!)* one Saturday afternoon.

This particular session hadn't gone well. We'd drunk a few cans and were losing our tempers. Dave had shouted at Gary, Gary had told Dave to sod off, they were his drums, it was his garage, and if Dave didn't like the way he played, he knew what he could do about it.

"Just try to keep to the beat!" Dave yelled. "And don't drown out the singer. That's all I'm asking. A child of two could do it!"

"Then get a child of two, mate. And take yourself and your poxy girlfriend out of here!"

Yes, indeed. Dave had persuaded Marie-Claire to come along and try out one of his songs with us, a pretty good number called *I'm leaving you now, babe.* I had strummed a few bars here and there and then sat back to listen to Marie-Claire: she had a nice voice, but not, whatever Dave might have thought, what it took to front a rock band. Anyhow, all the time she'd been singing, Gary had been crouched over his drums like a malevolent dwarf, glaring at the two of them and banging away as if he was trying to beat the skins to death. Either he fancied Marie-Claire himself and was putting the death wish on Dave, or we had underestimated his musical sensitivity and he didn't like the way she sang the song.

Maybe he just hated the thought of any two people getting it together.

"Come on, Gary." Dave tried to calm him down. "Let's give it another go."

"Go jump in the Liffey."

So Dave and I zipped our guitars into their cases, Marie-Claire zipped herself into her jacket and the three of us made a dignified exit.

"Come back to my place," Dave suggested. "Ma's out. I think. Anyway, she won't mind."

"I'll give it a miss," I said. I'd had enough of music for the day. And I was sure Dave would much prefer to be alone with Marie-Claire. *Come back and try out my lyrics:* it's an improvement on *Come and look at my etchings.* But not much.

It's not that I envied Dave. Not for trying to get off with Marie-Claire, anyway. She wasn't my type. *She wasn't my type*: the phrase trips off the tongue, doesn't it? What *was* my type? Rachel? No, not Rachel: I wasn't that much of a masochist. And did I even *have* a type? I know Marie-Claire didn't turn me on but, if she *had* taken a shine to me (yes, it's ludicrous I know, but princesses do have a history of fancying frogs), would I have become interested? Probably. I needed a girl, any girl, to kiss.

Thinking profound thoughts such as these, I wandered down to the park. It was quite pleasant out. The sun was shining, single people were walking their dogs, families were walking their kids, and couples . . . couples, joined like Siamese twins at the hand, at the hip, at the mouth, were everywhere reminding me of my unloved state. Even the drakes in the pond were ducking their ducks (good one that, Hugh) in a display of lust as shameless as that of the dogs mounting other people's bitches on the footpath.

The one discordant note was a figure huddled in a jacket, sitting miserably on the steps of the bandstand. Whoever it was looked as lonely and unloved as I felt myself. Or maybe, a cynical voice in my head suggested, it was just some kid completely out of it on drink. I looked for the tell-tale bottle of cheap cider.

I was just about to walk past when I realized it was Rachel.

"Rache! What are you doing here?"

She jumped. I caught a glimpse of a puffy, tear-stained face before she put her head down and let her hair fall over her face again. *Rachel? Crying?*

I sat down beside her. "What's up, Rache? Want to tell your Uncle Hughie all about it?"

She sniffed and hugged her knees even more tightly.

I tried out various sentences in my head: they all sounded naff. So I sat there silently, feeling a right prat, wondering whether to put an arm round her shoulders and give her a hug, thinking that she might take it the wrong way, wishing I'd got some lessons from Ma.

"Are you OK?" I asked finally. If that was the best I could come up with after so much thought, it was just as well I'd never wanted to work for any of the caring professions.

"It's not *fair*!" she muttered down at her knees. "We're *all* unhappy. Why do *I* have to be the only one who's trying to keep things together?"

I didn't know what she was talking about, so I shut up again. The strong, silent type, that's me.

"I'm fed up with staying in the house. And anyway, I had to see that Greenpeace woman about an article. Why shouldn't I be able just to go out for an hour without feeling so bloody guilty?"

"Mmm," I said.

"I know I should have brought Conor and Alice with me," she went on. "They need the fresh air. But you can't take a couple of little kids to an interview." She sniffed. Feeling like Cary Grant in one of these old movies, I went through my pockets for a clean handkerchief. Unsurprisingly, I didn't even have a tissue.

"Who's Conor and Alice?" I asked. Pathetic wasn't in it.

She slumped down on the wooden step again. "The twins."

I remembered the voices on the phone the one time I'd tried to ring her. "How old are they?"

"Six."

"And you're supposed to be minding them?" Well done, Holmes! Another case solved!

"No!" She sounded as if I'd accused her of armed robbery, of dropping litter, of being rude to whales. "*Josie*'s supposed to be minding them. But Josie's gone off with Peter, hasn't she?"

Had she? "Who's Josie?" This was beginning to sound like the Spanish Inquisition.

"My sister."

"So who's minding them instead, then?"

"Dad is. I *know* I shouldn't have left them with him, but they're *his* children, after all. Not mine. Why should *I* always be tied to the house, childminding, cleaning, shopping, cooking? It's just not fair."

Always? Was *that* why Rachel never came out with the rest of us? "What about . . . ? Where's . . . ?" How could I put the question without sounding crass?

"She's dead, if that's what you're trying to ask."

Oh, shit. "I'm sorry."

"Yeah. Thanks." This time she did get up. "I have to go."

"I'll come with you. It's on my way."

The normal Rachel would have picked up on that lie. This one didn't.

We left the park looking a couple like all the other couples. But we were two separate people, thinking our own separate thoughts. Mine were somewhat short of admirable. True, I wanted to help Rachel, wave a magic wand for her, make it all come right; but a part of me, a part I didn't like, was grinning away and rubbing its hands like mad. The great Rachel Cross is only human, it was chortling to itself; when push comes to shove, even a rabid feminist needs a man's support.

By the time we got to the park gates, Rachel had flicked a switch and was back to her old self. She started to talk about the newspaper. I went along with it. Even before we reached her house, I'd almost forgotten that I'd ever seen a different side to her.

She wouldn't let me come in. Said she was OK. As there were no ambulances with screaming sirens queuing up outside her front gate or smoke pouring out of a window, I assumed that all was well in the Cross household, despite her worries, and left her with a good conscience.

I found myself thinking about her, though, on the bus going home. Why hadn't she wanted me to go into her house? And why she was so worried about her little brother and sister? After all, she'd said her dad was at home and parents minded children: that was their job. It was also the job of parents to do the cooking and the cleaning and the shopping (well, most of it, anyhow), all the things that Rachel had been complaining about. Maybe for "parents", read "mothers", I thought. And Rachel's mum was dead.

I imagined Ma not being there. Even the most independent observer would have to admit she's a nag. She's always on my case about tidiness, good manners, self-discipline and all the rest of that garbage and we argue a lot. But if she wasn't around? Would Dad and me manage to keep the house going? Well, yes. Obviously. If we had to. But . . . I just couldn't imagine life without her. Mothers were *there* for you, when the chips were down. That's what mothers were for.

By the sound of it, Rachel was the mother in the Cross family now. Her and her sister – what was the sister's name? Josie.

Rachel needed rescuing, I told myself as I got off the bus. Sir Hugh O'Connor was going to polish up his suit of shining armour, take his trusty steed out of retirement and gallop off to save the damsel in distress!

I laughed out loud, causing a couple of lads in front of me to turn round in surprise. Rachel a damsel in distress who needed rescuing! Yeah, *right.* Rachel would eat Sir Lancelot with her organic cereal for breakfast.

But she'd been crying in the park. That new, vulnerable side to her had somehow got to me. I decided to forget my search for the perfect girl (which, let's face it, was going nowhere) and see more of Rachel, get to know her better.

There are near enough a thousand kids at our school and at least half of them are female. That makes over five hundred girls. And out of five hundred girls I had to choose Rachel Cross to take an interest in.

Chapter 14

It is my lady; O! it is my love:
O! that she knew she were.
Shakespeare, *Romeo and Juliet*

I rang Rachel the next day. This time, I wasn't going to take any excuses.

"Look, Rache, it's Sunday. You need a few hours to yourself. We can go for a walk or something."

"It's raining."

So it was. Typical. All these fine spring days and now, when I really wanted good weather, the heavens decided to start a second Flood. Sir Lancelot wouldn't have been put off by a bit of rain though; Sir Hugh wasn't going to be either. "OK, so we do something inside. Go bowling. See a film. *Something*. You need to get out of the house."

"How do you know what I need?"

This wasn't going exactly as I'd planned. I tried again: "*Everyone* needs to get out of the house. If you're looking after your little brother and sister all the time *and* cleaning and cooking and everything, you must need it more than most. Let somebody else do the work and come round here."

There was a silence at the other end.

"Come on, Rache. It's not normal for somebody your age to have to look after the family. Let whatsername, Josie, or your father . . ."

"Who are you to say what's normal and what's not? Who asked you to butt in?"

Shit. Why couldn't I choose my words more carefully? "I'm not butting in," I mumbled. "I just want to help."

"I don't need help."

Was Ma able to pick her way through all these verbal minefields? Did they give social workers courses in how to say the right thing? If so, it looked as if I'd have to go on a course myself if I wanted to get anywhere with Rachel. And I *did* want to get somewhere with her. It's amazing how a bit of mystery, not to mention playing-hard-to-get-ery can make you interested in someone.

"Listen, Rache," I began again. But the line was already dead.

I thought of turning up at her front door and confronting her father and/or big sister: "Rachel needs a break. I'm going to give her one. So get lost, mate – or mate-ess, as the case may be." I grinned at myself. What did I hope to do after that? Throw her over the bar of my bike and ride off with her into the sunset? Even if the sun *had* been shining, it wasn't on. First, I didn't have the guts. And more to the point, even if these articles you read in magazines are true and what most women *really* want is to be dragged out of the cave by a he-man in wolfskins with pectoral muscles you could use as flying saucers, even then I didn't think Rachel would be into it.

And, let's face it, my pectoral muscles leave a lot to be desired. As, obviously, did the rest of me.

Why is it we desire so much to be desired? Answer on one side of the paper only, please.

Rachel didn't come into school on Monday. I tried ringing in the evening but the phone seemed to be terminally engaged. If Josie was spending all evening talking to her beloved Pete, I hoped viciously that her dad would make her pay the phone bill.

On Tuesday Kate said that she was doing the layout of the paper herself that evening.

"What's the matter with Rachel?" I asked.

Kate shrugged: "I dunno. I guess she's sick. She rang my house last night when I was out and left a message."

So Rachel was ill. She could even have the flu, there was a lot of it about. That would explain the scene in the park: people get weepy with the flu. Don't they?

I convinced myself that that was all it was, nothing that couldn't be cured by a load of antibiotics and some vitamin pills. I rang again that Tuesday evening, all ready with sympathy and verbal get-well cards.

The phone was still engaged.

I tried again. And again. I even rang the phone company to see if there was a fault on the line.

The receiver was "off-hooked", they told me.

What did that mean? My first thought, I'm ashamed to admit, was a cross between *Psycho* and *The Silence of the Lambs:* someone was in the house holding the whole family hostage! Before I called the police, though, I saw sense and realised that I was letting my imagination run as wild as Marie-Claire's. So the phone was off-hooked? What was so frightening about that? Maybe Rachel was sleeping and her dad didn't want the phone to wake her up.

Once I had started worrying, though, I found that I couldn't stop. And, worse than that, my imagination had started to go beyond flu, even beyond horror films. Every newspaper you read these days reveals a new case of child abuse or incest – was *that* why Rachel kept so much to herself and why her moods changed so suddenly? It was all Marie-Claire's fault, I decided. If she hadn't suggested that there was something wrong with Rachel's home life, I wouldn't be biting my nails like this. And don't ask me why I was letting myself be influenced by Marie-Claire *now*, when I'd taken the piss just as much as Dave in the past. Is that what getting interested in a girl does for you? Rots your common sense?

There was nothing wrong in Rachel's home, I told myself firmly, except that she didn't have a mother. Other people didn't have mothers and they coped. And Rachel was the best person at coping I knew. If she had the flu now it might do the rest of the family good: they would have to learn how to manage without her.

I stopped trying to ring her, watched some telly and went to bed.

Chapter 15

A journeyman printer of the sixteenth century in Europe worked twelve to sixteen hours a day, printing from 2,500 to 3,500 sheets.

Wednesday afternoon came and the weekly session with the photocopier. There was still no sign of Rachel.

Kate dropped by the office and handed the pasted-up spreads to Marie-Claire and myself, saying: "Sorry I can't stay." Before I had time to open my mouth, she was gone. Like Rachel, Kate thought that she never had to explain herself: it must come with the how-to-be-a-feminist information pack.

The reason Marie-Claire and I were alone in the office was that Dave was having a tête-à-tête with Frankenstein (something to do with the fact that he'd been caught, *again,* bunking off games – he'll never learn), and Kerry hadn't turned up.

"I don't know about you," I muttered, as I folded page after page of photocopied A2 sheets, trying to keep them in the right order. "This newspaper was supposed to be *fun*. If you work out the time we spend doing this, not to mention the time it takes to research and write our articles, it's worse than studying for eight honours in the Leaving Cert."

"Don't you get a buzz, though, seeing your stuff in print?"

"Yeah. I suppose." I folded a few more sheets. "Tell me, have you ever been to Rachel's house?" I asked casually.

"No." She didn't seem to find my sudden change of subject strange. "Rachel's not really into the best-pals, girly scene. She's a very private person. You have to respect that."

"Don't you mind that Kate's always going round there?"

"Not always," she corrected me. "Only once a week to work on the paper. They need time and space to set it all out and do the illustrations and see where everything fits in."

I wondered, not for the first time, if Marie-Claire was really so good-natured, deep down. Didn't she feel hurt at all? I wouldn't have blamed her if she had done. After all, she and Rachel had been friends, in as much as Rachel had been friends with anyone, before Kate came along.

We worked away for a while in a relaxed silence. To get the 200-plus newspapers we were selling a week now, we had to photocopy both sides of over 400 A2 sheets, put the inner spread inside the outer, and fold each newspaper down the middle, *by hand*. When there were a few of us at it, it wasn't too bad. With just two, it seemed to last a lifetime.

"Kate is more Rachel's type, anyway," Marie-Claire said, a few minutes later. "She's intellectual, like Rache. I mean, Rachel wouldn't have anything in common with Kerry and me, not really. That sounds bitchy," she corrected herself quickly, "I didn't mean it like that. I admire both of them, really I do."

Did she *ever* stop being nice about people?

"You know that her mother's dead?" I asked.

"Oh, yes. She died last summer. In a car accident. Miss O'Brien, our form mistress, told us all about it the first day back in September – so that we could be nice to Rachel, I suppose." She smiled: "You can imagine how mad that made her."

I could. Rachel reminded me of a hedgehog, trundling along OK, getting on with its life, until someone comes too close; then it curls up into a ball and shows its prickles.

"I worry about her," I said. "She seems to spend all her time minding her little brother and sister. And keeping house and everything. It's not natural. What does her father do?"

"He's a teacher."

That wasn't what I meant. But it made the situation even more weird. Why did her dad do nothing about the house, *especially* if he was a teacher? My Dad's an accountant and never stops going on about the hours teachers work and the holidays they have. "If he's a teacher, he has plenty of time to do his share. Or he could pay to get a housekeeper in. Why should it all land on Rachel?"

Marie-Claire frowned. "D'you remember what I said the last time we talked about Rache? That time I met you and Dave in town? You thought I was crazy, but maybe I'm right after all."

Did I remember? I'd been thinking of nothing else for days. But it was one thing to think it in an academic, what-if sort of a way; quite another to talk about it as a possible fact. "No! No way!" I was surprised at how strongly I answered her. "You've got it all wrong. And anyway, you just said her father's a teacher. I mean, we're talking Rachel here, not some down-and-out from a slum family on the dole!"

"Why are you getting so upset, Hugh?" Marie-Claire asked quietly.

"I'm not," I blustered. "It's just . . . You're just . . . I mean . . ."

"Abuse happens in all types of families. Don't you ever read the papers?"

"Yeah, I know. But not Rachel!" Rachel the feminist. Rachel the no-nonsense epitome of self-assertiveness. Rachel who wouldn't even talk to me on the telephone. Marie-Claire was way out of line.

She seemed to feel that herself. "I could be wrong," she admitted.

"You *are* wrong," I told her. "I don't know why her father doesn't do his bit at home, but it's not that. Rachel would have mentioned something."

"Would she? She never talks about anything personal."

"She did to me. On Saturday." And I told Marie-Claire about the scene in the park. "I mean, it's probably because of her family that she's not been in school this week. Or, if she's got the flu, she probably only caught it because she's killing herself trying to be a mother to everybody *and* come to school *and* run this poxy newspaper. I'm getting fed up with it myself," I kicked the pile of newspapers we'd already folded – a bad move, that, as I then had to do half of them all over again, "and I don't have all the extra stress she has."

Marie-Claire looked thoughtful. "I'll ring her tonight," she said. "Maybe we can give her a hand. Or get help for her."

"You won't get through. Her phone's off the hook or something. And I wouldn't suggest getting help," I warned her. "You know what Rachel's like."

Did I really believe that, once Marie-Claire had the bit between her teeth, she'd not charge in like a bull (a cow?) in a china shop?

I tried myself to get in touch with Rachel again that evening. This time the phone rang. And rang. I held on.

Finally: "Yes?" It sounded like Rachel's voice.

"It's me. Hugh. I just wanted to – "

The phone was banged down, cutting me off in mid-speech.

I stood there looking at the receiver. What had I done? On Saturday, I was Hugh the Hero; today, she slams the phone down on me.

She was sick, I told myself. And under stress. Us knights in shining armour have to make allowances. So I wandered back into the front room, picked up the cat and settled down with it to watch the box.

To my surprise, Rachel turned up in the canteen at lunch-time the next day. She didn't look as I'd expected, all pale and wan and fragile. In fact, she looked like Boadicea about to annihilate a Roman legion single-handed – or like Queen Maebh just after her husband's told her that his bull is better than hers. She stamped over to where Dave and I were sitting.

"Thanks," she spat at me. "Thanks a lot."

Dave looked up in surprise. "Is there something going on here that I'm missing?"

She ignored him. "In future, I'd be grateful if you'd kindly stop gossiping about my private life to everyone you meet. Do I make myself clear?"

Marie-Claire! I thought. "I didn't gossip," I protested. "I only mentioned to Marie-Claire that I was worried about you . . ."

"Well, don't be. I can manage fine on my own, thank you. I do not need the Samaritans, nor a counsellor, nor a shrink. I am quite all right. Have you got that? Good."

She turned and stalked off. Trust Marie-Claire to go over the top. I wondered what the hell she'd said on the phone. I looked round the room: Marie-Claire was at the other side of the canteen, with Kerry. She smiled apologetically and shrugged.

"What was all that about?" Dave wanted to know.

"Nothing," I said.

I knew my face was as red as the ketchup on the table.

Why had I ever thought I could get anywhere with Rachel? Why had I even bothered? Just because she had been human one afternoon, I'd thought she was worth getting to know better. I'd asked her out. I'd even been willing to *help* her. And what did I get in return? She ignores me for days, slams down the phone on me and then treats me like a bit of slime in front of my friends.

It was too much. In future, I decided, our acquaintance would be limited to working together on the newspaper. As for her private life, she could continue to be a martyr to her family if she wanted; I wasn't going to get involved.

And I was certainly never going to ask her out, ever again.

Chapter 16

Will you, won't you, will you, won't you, will you join the dance?

Lewis Carroll: *Alice's Adventures in Wonderland*

I didn't ask Rachel out again. Not immediately. Not until after the St Patrick's Disco.

The St Patrick's Disco is one of the biggest events in the Monkscross Comprehensive social calendar. Transition Year organises it every year, having nothing better to do with itself.

Kerry and Marie-Claire were, naturally, both on the committee and were really keen.

"We could decorate the gym all in shamrocks . . . no, that might be a bit tacky, what do you think?"

"What about green, orange and white streamers and balloons?"

"Nah. Bo-ring. I know, snakes! Snakes climbing up and down the wallbars and hanging from the beam, vines all over the place . . ."

"That's jungles. There wouldn't have been vines in Ireland even in St Patrick's time, would there?"

"What? Oak forests with wolves? You're slagging, Dave.

Will you stop prancing around, howling like that! Can't you be serious for a minute? This is important."

In the end they decided to have everything green. "We're going to scrounge a whole pile of old sheets and dye them," Kerry told us proudly. "You won't recognise the place – it'll look magic!"

Magic was one word for it. Gross would have been another. "Ouch!" Dave winced as we stepped through the gym door into a green tent.

"Leprechauns of the world unite?" I suggested.

"St Patrick's Purgatory?"

"Interior design for a Martian flying saucer?"

The Martian effect was added to by the number of people who had taken the committee's request to wear green seriously and were not only dressed in green from head to toe but had dyed their hair and painted their faces to match. Dave, not surprisingly, was one of these. He bore a certain resemblance to a stick of celery, something I wasn't quite tactful enough to hide from him.

"And you think you look smart, do you, in that polka-dot bow tie? Not to mention the waistcoat? What did I do with my shades?" He took a step back and put a hand up to shield his eyes; he was a real loss to the amateur dramatic circuit.

We leaned up against the green-covered wall bars and looked around for Marie-Claire or anyone else from our gang. "Where are they all?" Dave asked peevishly. "*They*'re supposed to be here waiting for us. *We*'re supposed to be the ones that are late."

"Did nobody ever tell you there's been a new dispensation?"

"A new what?"

Then Louise came by, looking sexy in floating green net over a green low-cut dress. (I thought of the gentlewomen of Verona: had she been raiding the props cupboard?) "Hi!"

"You seen Marie-Claire?" Dave asked. Straight to the point as ever.

"She's helping get the food ready backstage. She'll be out in a minute – we're just about there."

"Oh shit, food!" Dave and I looked at each other. The girls had made it very clear that *everyone* was supposed to bring something, sandwiches, sausage rolls, whatever, as our year was running the thing. Ah well, win a few, lose a few. Dave and I had been too busy thinking about drink to remember about food.

Not that we'd any success with the drink, either. We'd arranged to meet at my place for a couple of cans before the dance, to get us in the mood, but Dad had cleared all the beer out of the fridge.

Ma had caught us just as we were opening the door to look for it. She must have been hiding in a cupboard or something: mothers can be unbelievably devious at times.

"Lost anything, you two?" she'd asked sweetly.

"Just looking for a yoghurt," I'd lied.

"Lager-flavoured, no doubt." She'd sighed. Mothers are good at sighing; it makes you think they bear all the troubles of the world. "You're both too young to drink, you know that as well as I do. Does it never cross your minds that there's something sad in having to give yourselves Dutch courage every time you go out somewhere?"

"It's not every time. And we don't need courage, Dutch, Irish or Japanese. We were just looking for yoghurt, like I said. It must be terrible for you, having such a suspicious mind."

Ma had smiled even more sweetly. "It is, believe me. I sometimes wonder myself *why* I have one. Could it be because I have you for a son?"

Anyhow, we'd made a quick getaway but had forgotten all

about the food. Well, nobody really expects food at these things, do they?

As we waited for Marie-Claire, I wondered if the girls had been able to get Rachel to come. It was unlikely – discos were hardly her scene.

So I was surprised when I saw her at the other side of the gym. And it wasn't just the fact that she'd turned up at a school disco that blew my mind.

She was dancing with Mr Bronson, our PE teacher, and was wearing – wait for it! – black shiny trousers, a white shirt with a green silk scarf tucked into the neck of it and (remember we're talking about *Rachel* here) an emerald-green cape lined with black. She had her hair loose (she usually wore it tied back) and, as she danced, it seemed to flame, tawny gold, against the green of her cape. The cape swirled around her, her hair flew across her face and she looked positively beautiful. Rachel beautiful? It had never occurred to me before.

"Wow!" Dave said. "Is that our Rache?" He gave a low whistle.

"Take your eyes off my woman," I said automatically. "Stick to your own."

As if on cue, Marie-Claire came out from behind the stage carrying a plate of sandwiches. She looked stunning too. Most of her (well, at least half of her) was wrapped in a clinging green dress and her legs seemed about five miles long. Kerry was with her. Even from where we were, you could see that Kerry was talking away, a thousand to the dozen as usual, and Marie-Claire was listening as if she was really interested. She was the only one of us who had the patience. "She's a nice girl, Marie-Claire," I said.

"Nice? Is that all you can say about her? What's happened to your red blood corpuscles? Or has Rachel sucked you dry, like a vegetarian vampire?" Dave made kissing noises. "Marie-Claire is a wonder of the western world, Monkscross's answer to page three of the *Sun*, and tonight she is going to be mine." He started to cross the gym towards her. "Don't wait up for me, Hughie darling," he drawled over his shoulder. "I may be gone some time."

I thought of writing a letter myself to the next edition of the paper: *Dear Auntie Mabel, I think my best friend is a total prat. What should I do about it?*

I copped myself on. What was happening to me? Was Dave right and was Rachel affecting my judgement – despite the fact that I had no interest in her whatsoever? I'd even found myself criticising my mother's choice of washing powder the other day. Washing powder! I'd told Ma that the powder she normally bought was bad for the environment and she should be using an environmentally-friendly one; she'd told me *I* could use what *I* wanted whenever *I* did the washing (a nasty dig that, Ma can be quite shameless at times) but that *she* wanted to get *her* wash clean; I'd said that the other stuff *did* get your wash clean (well, Rachel never looked dirty, did she?); she'd said it was all a scam; I'd told her that she had no social conscience . . . Mind you, I notice that she has changed her powder (*and* her washing-up liquid *and* her toilet-cleaner), so maybe Rachel's got a point.

I'd also decided to go vegetarian. Well, to a certain extent, anyway. It was one of Rachel's articles on farming methods that persuaded me. I mean, once you know how battery chickens are kept, you can't sit down to Sunday dinner with a good conscience any more. I would be waiting impatiently as Dad started to carve, my saliva ducts on overtime, my knife and fork poised, and then the gleaming golden bird on the plate in the middle of the table would, right before my eyes as they say, metamorphose into a featherless, crazy-eyed, poultry-concentration-camp-inmate, staring piteously at me through the bars of its tiny wire cage. And I just couldn't eat it.

Eventually the dance came to an end and Bronson led Rachel off the floor. I pushed my way through the crowd towards her.

"Hi, Rache. You look great." Silver-tongued, that's me; just the man to come up with a brand new earthshattering compliment. Yes.

Rachel smiled.

I straightened my green bow tie and bowed. "Would *madame* care to join me in this dance?"

She bowed back, spreading out her cape. "*Madame* would be delighted."

We found a space and shuffled about for a while. Rachel had a surprisingly good sense of rhythm. I decided to be adventurous and tried moving around a bit more. She did the same. We got a little space for ourselves on the gym floor and started to have a good time.

It was a great evening. I danced a lot with Rachel, Dave danced a lot with Marie-Claire. Sometimes we swopped around, and I think both of us danced with Kate a couple of times. All the newspaper crowd was there, Louise and Brian seemed to have become a couple (though what she could see in him was a mystery to me), and Kerry had found her fifth-year jock and was blind to the rest of the world.

At one stage I was having a break, leaning against the wall, watching Marie-Claire and Dave, Rachel and Brian bopping away under the green strobe lights and thinking deep philosophical thoughts (like whether or not I could persuade Rachel to let me walk her home at the end of the evening and, if I did, whether I'd get any further with her this time than the last. OK, so I'd changed my mind about not getting involved. That's allowed, isn't it?), when someone spoke to me:

"Not a great crowd, is there?"

I looked up. Gleeson was standing beside me, eying the talent.

"Nuh," I muttered, unsticking myself from the wall bars, ready to move away.

"Mind you," Gleeson went on, "it's quality not quantity that counts. And that little Hannigan girl is quite something, isn't she?"

Marie-Claire was still dancing with Dave, managing to look as if she was enjoying it despite Dave's manic antics.

"She's wasted on Dave Westmore," Gleeson announced. "Someone should do something about it."

"How's Mrs Gleeson?" I asked, managing to sound cold and casual but annoyed to feel myself blushing.

Gleeson wasn't fazed. "She's fine, thank you, Hugh," he said urbanely. "As are the children. I didn't know you cared."

I tried to think of a cutting reply. You never can, though, when you really need one.

"Yes . . . she's a looker indeed," Gleeson practically stroked the words. "Excuse me, Hugh. I think the time has come to rescue the fair Juliet from the cavortings of our erstwhile Romeo there. You young things ought to learn that it is possible to dance properly, even to this excuse for real music." And, before I could say anything, or trip him up, or pull a green sheet down on top of his head, he was pushing his way across the gym to Marie-Claire.

I watched, hoping Dave would stamp on his toes. Or bash him one in the eye with a flailing elbow. He did try to argue, I could see that from where I was standing, but Gleeson just cut in, as he'd done at the post-play party, and waltzed Marie-Claire off, leaving poor Dave in the middle of the floor looking like a tall green hairy wally.

He came over to where I was standing. "Did you see that?" He looked ready to punch someone.

"Yeah. Why did you let him get away with it? You know Marie-Claire can't stand the guy."

Dave looked embarrassed. "He's a teacher, isn't he? What was I suppose to do? Sock him one? *Unhand my damsel, sirrah, or I'll kick your head in!* I'm not into contact sports."

We watched Marie-Claire dance with Gleeson. He had his arms round her and she didn't look happy.

"We have to do something!" Dave moaned.

But Marie-Claire beat us to it herself. We saw her shove Gleeson away, say something to him, Gleeson laying a hand on her arm, Marie-Claire pushing him off; and then she was coming through the crowd towards us, her face white.

"Let's go," she said to Dave.

"OK."

Rachel appeared. "What's going on?" she asked. "I saw you fighting off Creepy Chris. Are you all right?"

"Yes," Marie-Claire said. "I've had enough, though. I'm going home."

Rachel looked back at the dance floor: Gleeson had disappeared. "It makes me mad to let a sleaze like him drive us away."

"The rest of you don't have to come."

"It's OK. It's time I thought of getting home, anyway."

"Fine, then," I said. "Let's all get out of here."

We found our coats and headed for the door. Gleeson was there before us, stamping people's hands, looking as innocent as a newborn babe. Or as a fully paid-up member of the teachers' union.

"You got stamped, all of you?" he asked. "You won't get back in, otherwise."

Marie-Claire avoided looking at him. Dave and Rachel glared. I gave him a filthy look.

He just smiled and waved us through the door.

"The bastard!" Dave muttered once we were outside. "The smarmy git! If I could just get hold of him . . ."

"Ah, leave him be. He's not worth it." That, of course, was Marie-Claire.

Chapter 17

For kissing his wife in public on a Sunday after just returning from a three-year voyage, a Boston ship captain was made to sit two hours in stocks, two hundred years ago, for "lewd and unseemely behaviour."

A couple contemplating kissing or holding hands in public should be advised that the Minnesota Department of Education has issued guidelines warning the state's public school students not to engage in "displays of affection in hallways," on the grounds that such displays "may offend others" and are "heterosexist."

Sex and Dating, The Official Politically Correct Guide,
Beard & Cerf, HarperCollins

I kissed Rachel last night. Wow!

It had been after ten when we'd come out of the disco. There isn't a lot to do after 10 pm on a Saturday night in the middle of March when you're too young to get into a pub. So we went to Dave's house, which is nearest the school.

We sat in his kitchen, made ourselves toasted cheese sandwiches, drank cocoa (this was certainly an alcohol-free evening – Ma would have been delighted) and listened to music.

Some of the tapes were ones Dave had recorded in Gary's garage with the band: bits of them didn't sound too bad but other bits made me squirm. Especially with Rachel listening. I avoided her eye and, tactfully, she kept her mouth shut.

She hadn't wanted to come, but Marie-Claire had talked her into it. And all the time she was with us she was looking at her watch. Ma could be strict about curfews but Mr Cross must be out of the ark, I remember thinking.

When she finally stood up and said she was going, I offered to see her home. Yes, I know I had decided I wasn't going to bother with her any more and here I was, right back to being . . . well, curious about her. Not to mention caring about her. All right, to feeling that every atom and molecule in my body was totally and utterly aware of her, in a way I'd never been aware of anyone before.

The fact that she was willing to let me come back to her house with her was a start. But I never expected to us get any further, not once she began to go on about Gleeson again.

"Can't we give it a rest, Rache? It's Saturday night." I waved extravagantly towards the moon, hanging in the sky above the dark, castle-topped silhouette of Dalkey Hill: "The moon's in her heaven and all's right with the world. Why bring Gleeson into it?"

"OK," she said, surprising me. "Think of something else to talk about."

I thought. Nothing intellectual enough to impress Rachel came to mind. The political situation? I didn't know enough about it. The economy? Likewise. Music? Art? Literature? My mind was a complete blank. I remembered reading somewhere about some recent book prize, but could I think of a single author now? I decided to take refuge in my usual brand of corny humour: "OK," I said. "The price of cheese."

"What about it?"

"Talk for one minute on *The price of cheese*."

She laughed. "All right. If bread is the staff of life, cheese is the pointy bit at the end. Bread and cheese go together like . . . like . . ."

"A horse and carriage?"

"That's love and marriage. Anyway, when did you last see a horse and carriage?"

"When did you last see love going with marriage?" I countered.

If anyone ever invents a mechanism for taking things back before you've said them, they'd make a fortune. I mentally kicked myself: what was it Marie-Claire had said? Rachel's mother had died only last summer. And I make cheap cracks about marriage.

There was a moment's silence while I prayed for the pavement to open up and swallow me. Then, brightly, she picked up the thread of her "talk": "Which is why it is so immoral to inflate the price of cheese, thus taking wholesome food from the mouths of the poor. Anyway, I don't know if I believe that too much love in a marriage is such a good thing."

That last bit was added on so seamlessly that I almost let it pass; and then I heard it properly, like the echo of a sound you don't catch the first time. Was she giving me a chance to talk about her problems at home? If she was, I messed up again.

"That's OK by me. I wasn't actually planning to propose tonight. Just to swear my undying love."

She didn't smile. "Do you think there's such a thing as undying love?"

"I dunno. Poets go on about it all the time. And my old gran and granda are still together after," I put on a quavery voice, "nigh on sixty years." Hugh O'Connor, the class clown. Why couldn't I be serious for once?

"Too much love can be dangerous," she said. She sounded bitter.

"What's the matter, Rache? Would it help to talk about it?" I sounded like Ma with one of her clients.

"Talking doesn't help." Her voice came out all small, as if she was close to tears.

Without even thinking what I was doing, I took her in my arms (no, that sounds too like a romantic novel: *the firm-jawed hero took the quivering maiden into his arms . . .*) I pulled her towards me and held her, like you'd cuddle a little kid who's hurt itself.

She snuggled her head into my shoulder and sniffed. I have to admit, it felt good. There's something to this protective he-man stuff after all.

I patted her back and had the sense to stay silent. (*The strong silent hero . . .* Forget it!) I was reminded of the time I'd come across her on the bandstand at the park. Was our relationship (our what? I heard Dave ask) always going to be based on me being nothing more than a handy shoulder to cry on? Mind you, I still found the whole idea of Rachel crying . . . what? shocking? surprising, anyway. There must be something very wrong in her life somewhere; or else her feminist self-confidence was just an act, in which case she was the best actress I'd ever seen.

It was intriguing. Was this why I found her so interesting? But she also looked quite different tonight, all dressed up for the disco. Pretty. Sexy, even. Although I genuinely found myself wanting to protect this new vulnerable Rachel, my nerve ends were jangling too. I wondered what she would be like to kiss.

Shall I be honest? Why not? Isn't that what all this is about? OK, then, here goes: what I really wondered was what *it* would be like to kiss. And I mean *really* kiss, not the pecks on the cheek you give someone like your ma or your auntie, or even the odd (some of them *very* odd) tries we've all had with various more-or-less willing accomplices since about fourth class in National School. Go on, laugh if you want. But I'd led a sheltered life, hadn't I?

Just as I was working out how to get our lips together (that was another lesson, Ms Blenchley: I've discovered how easy it is to be both caring and calculating at the same time), Rachel raised her head. At least she had stopped crying.

"I think I'd better go home."

We came apart, but I held on to her hand. She didn't try to pull it away. Walking hand in hand with a girl doesn't happen to me very often. In fact, and I hope you're impressed at how honest I'm being about this, apart from Teresa Brennon in sixth class and Julie Thompson last year (which lasted all of four days), the only girl I've walked hand in hand with regularly has been my little cousin. And that's only to stop her running under a bus when I'm told to take her to the park.

Holding Rachel's hand was different. *Totally* different.

We reached her house. How could I keep her a few minutes longer? I put an arm round her again and gave her a hug. "Are you OK? You sure you don't want to tell me what's wrong?"

"Thanks, Hugh." She pulled away and opened her gate. "There's nothing wrong, nothing I can't handle. Goodnight." And she kissed me. On the cheek.

Huh! I can hear you saying. Is that it?

It would be nice to be able to say that I was masterful, all of a sudden, and pulled her into my strong manly arms; but it didn't happen like that. Just, suddenly, we were kissing. *Properly*. And it was great.

She stopped first. We moved apart. In the light of the street lamp, I could see that she was smiling. "Well!" she said.

"When can I see you again?"

"School on Monday?"

"What about tomorrow?"

"I'm sorry." She sounded genuine. "I promised I'd take the twins to the zoo."

"Sunday, then?" But I remembered that we were all going up to Belfast for the day to visit Uncle Phelim and Auntie Dorothy. There was no way I could get out of it.

"Or, better still, why don't I come to the zoo with you tomorrow?"

She hesitated. "All right, then."

And that was that.

We fixed a time to meet and I watched her go into the darkened house. I stayed in the street, not caring about the cold, and waited till the lights went on, first in the hall and then in her bedroom. And that was when I remembered the last time I'd stood there – and Marie-Claire's suspicions.

No! Marie-Claire had an over-active imagination. She should stick to writing love stories, I told myself. Rachel was only upset because of her mother and the house was only dark because her dad liked to economise on electricity.

That settled, I walked home on air.

Chapter 18

The heterosexual couple is the basic unit of the political structure of male supremacy. In it each individual woman comes under the control of an individual man. It is more efficient than keeping women in ghettoes, camps, or even sheds at the bottom of the garden.

Leeds Revolutionary Feminist group, quoted in *Sex and Dating, The Official Politically Correct Guide,* Beard & Cerf, HarperCollins

It was sunny the next morning, quite unusual for a St Patrick's weekend really, and Dave rang suggesting we went somewhere with the girls. "We could cycle up to Powerscourt Waterfall. Take a picnic."

"Sorry. Count me out."

"What? Don't tell me you're scared of asking Rabid Rache? Has she managed to reduce you to a quivering heap of politically correct jelly with one stamp of her hobnailed Docs?"

"Don't call her that."

"What? Rabid Rache? Why not? And why are you rushing to her protection, all of a sudden? The day that Rachel Cross needs a man to protect her . . ." He broke off. I could practically hear the thoughts going through his head at the other end of the line. "So that's it! What happened last night then, eh?"

"Nothing happened. I just have things to do today. That's all."

"Mmm. Remember, ve have vays of making you talk. You can keep no secrets from me."

"Your accent stinks."

"Compliments will get you nowhere."

This time I went silent.

"OK," Dave said. "Have it your own way. Me and Marie-Claire will go off on our own. As long as you realise that, if anything happens, it'll all be your fault."

"Chance would be a fine thing," I told him. "Have a nice time."

I've got to admit that it surprised me, too, that I'd fallen for Rachel. As I rummaged in my wardrobe for a decent sweater (yes! Ma was right: all I needed was the love of a good woman to reform my slovenly ways), I marvelled at how quickly it had all happened. One moment I had decided I didn't want to have anything more to do with her, the next we were going out on a date together (OK, along with the terrible twins but, even so, it was a date). And I was really looking forwards to seeing her again!

There was more to Rachel than feminism. She was an interesting girl. Intelligent. Principled. And sexy. Well, she turned me on. She was good-looking too, when she bothered. And given that I myself am not exactly an oil painting (even Ma, who sometimes seems less doting than mothers ought to be on their one and only sons, admits that), I couldn't really object to my girlfriend being somewhat more . . . er . . . cuddly than was strictly in fashion.

OK, I've said it: my girlfriend. My girlfriend, Rachel Cross.

It's a strange old world, all right.

So there we were at the zoo, having survived two bus journeys without losing (or killing) either Conor or Alice.

I'm not that used to young children. Rachel managed just fine, but I found it a bit of a pain looking after a couple of under-age hooligans who ran up and down the bus, changed from one seat to another and made loud remarks like: "Rachel, is that a man or a woman?" "Rachel, why has that lady got hair on her chin? Is she a witch?" or "Rachel, there's a man smoking in the back seat. Shall I tell the driver?"

Fortunately, they behaved better at the zoo. Mostly because their mouths were continually stuffed with ice-cream, popcorn and sweets, but also because they had more room to run around in. They were like a couple of untrained puppies: if they left us alone for a couple of minutes to go off and look at something, they'd come tearing back almost immediately to pull at our arms: "We're hungry, buy us something," "We want to see the snakes," "We're tired, carry us."

Rachel and I held hands and talked. Yes, I know: you're expecting a steamy sex scene here – or a bit of a snog behind the penguin enclosure at the very least. All right, so it crossed my mind. But there wasn't much I could do about it with the twins running round us all the time, was there?

As the afternoon wore on, I realized that I was doing most of the talking while Rachel listened. And I was telling her all about myself while she was giving practically nothing back.

"That's enough about me. You say something now." I held an imaginary microphone in front of her. "Rachel Cross: This is Your Life!"

She just smiled.

"Come on now, Miss Cross," I prompted. "You were born . . ."

"I was born, I live, one day I'll die. End of story."

"Well, yes." I tried again. "There must be more." I swept my arm round to include the geese and ducks waddling across the grass, the wallabies hopping about in the paddock, the flamingos standing on one leg in the pond. "Your audience is waiting!"

"Hey, look! They're just about to feed the sea lions. Come on, you two." She rounded up Alice and Conor. "Let's go!"

And that was that.

The weather got worse. The sun found it had more interesting business elsewhere, the temperature dropped about ten degrees and it started to rain. We went into the cafeteria to get warm. It was packed, as everyone else had come in to shelter too. We got a table and bought Coke and chocolate biscuits for the twins (a mistake, that: they managed to smear chocolate all over themselves, the table, the chairs – and probably most of the toilet when Rachel took them there to clean them up).

"You won't guess who's at a table over there," she said as she brought them back.

"You're right. I won't." I did my straight-man act: "Who is at a table over there?"

"Gleeson and family. Daddy Gleeson, Mammy Gleeson and all the little Gleesons."

"*All* the little Gleesons? Not *all* the little Gleesons!"

She grinned. "Don't knock it: there are about a hundred of them. Well, at least six. I didn't want to stare."

I stood up. "Excuse me a moment. I need to see a man about a dog."

The twins giggled.

I weaved my way across the room. There was a load of carroty heads just to the left of the toilet doors. Hiding behind a stand of postcards, I spied on them. Two tables had been pushed together to make one bigger table and Gleeson himself was sitting, fortunately with his back to me, at the near end. He had a red-haired baby in his arms. At the far end, opposite him, a middle-aged hippy-looking woman with long hair tied back in a pony-tail was trying to sort out a war between two kids who were dismembering a plastic dinosaur. The table itself was covered with empty crisp bags, half-chewed cakes, paper cups and puddles of spilt drink. And round it sat, I counted, five carroty-haired kids of various sizes as well as the baby on Gleeson's lap and three non-red-haired girls all much about the same age as the eldest carrot-head. Maybe it was her birthday party?

I knew Gleeson had a wife and family. He'd admitted as much at the school disco the night before. But that he was responsible for all this! Six miniature Gleesons! The mind, as they say, boggled.

Why is it always so strange to find that teachers have lives of their own out of school?

When I got back to our table, Rachel was standing up and the twins had already escaped to chase a peacock across the *(Don't walk on the grass!)* lawn outside. We sneaked out of the cafeteria, trying not to look at Gleeson's table, hoping to avoid being seen. With luck, he had enough on his plate, both metaphorically and literally, not to notice us.

Gathering up the twins, we walked hand in hand (in hand in hand: if I wanted to hold hands with Rachel, I had to hold hands with Alice, too, while Rachel took hold of Conor on the other side) to the bus stop.

We went upstairs on the bus. As the twins fought for which of them was going to sit beside the window in the seat in front of us, I put my arm round Rachel's shoulders.

"There's a turn-up for the books," I said. "Gleeson the family man."

"It doesn't excuse him for being a lech."

I left it there. The twins had stopped squabbling and were falling asleep: I had Rachel to myself at last.

I pulled her closer and kissed her hair. It smelt nice. "Mmm," she said, sounding almost as drowsy as the twins. Me and Rachel Cross! I couldn't help thinking. If only Dave could see us now!

But when I tried to turn her face round to kiss her properly, she pushed me away. "Not now, Hugh."

"Why? Because someone might see?" I slagged. Rachel was the last person I could imagine worrying about what other people would think.

"The twins might wake up. And . . ." She hesitated. "I don't think I want any more complications in my life at the moment."

"Huh," I said. "So that's what I am? A complication? And I was thinking I was the love of your life." Automatically, I'd made a joke of it. I should have asked her what she meant. Or told her that it *hurt* to be thought of as just a complication (although that was marginally better than being only a handy shoulder to cry on). Why didn't I? Because real men don't whinge?

She didn't answer, anyway. In fact, the nearer we got to her stop, the cooler she became. I couldn't understand it. She'd been happy enough to kiss me the evening before, she'd seemed *pleased* that I'd wanted to go to the zoo with her, and she'd had no problem with me holding her hand or hugging her, either there or on the bus home. Until now.

Every time I touched her, I felt a tingle like an electric shock going right through me. I'd thought she'd been feeling the same way. Was love, as the song goes, just a one-way street?

We got off the bus and walked to her house. "Wait a minute," I said as we reached her gate.

"What is it, Hugh? Can't it keep? I'm late already." She sounded impatient.

I was tempted to leave it there. Us O'Connors don't throw ourselves at women who don't want us. But I thought I'd give her another chance.

"I just want to talk to you for a moment."

Alice and Conor were hovering on the steps. Rachel smiled at them. "In you go, you two. Wash your hands and then set the table. I won't be a minute."

They opened the door and disappeared.

"Well? What is it? I have to go in."

"I thought you liked me," I said. Pathetically.

Rachel groaned. "I do. But now's not the time. I have to check if Josie's in and see if she's made the tea." She smiled and my insides turned to water. Then she stood on her toes and kissed my cheek. You've got it: we were back to pecks-on-the-cheek again.

I grabbed her. "Come out later, then. We could go to a film."

She pushed me away. Gently but firmly, as they say. "No. I can't. Sorry, Hugh."

"When can we talk, then?"

"Next week. I'll see you in school." She looked anxiously up at the house. It stared steadily back: if it was going to blow up or burn down or disappear in a puff of smoke, it wasn't letting on.

"I *have* to go, Hugh. But I *will* see you in school on Monday. Enjoy Belfast tomorrow."

And the door was shut in my face.

Chapter 19

> The annual expenditure of the United Nations is only £6.6 billion, for all its peacekeeping and relief operations and everything else, from organising the Law of the Sea to training millions of teachers and nurses in developing countries. That is less than Americans spend in a year on cut flowers and pot plants. It is £1.2 per human being alive on Earth. Governments' military expenditure is still about £90 per human being.

> Every year in the US four times the amount of money spent on baby food is spent on pet food.

And that was the way the relationship went along. She seemed to like being with me. But whenever I tried to get closer to her, a door slammed shut.

Give her time, I told myself. It was only a few months, really, since she'd lost her mother – she was probably still grieving, even if she didn't know it herself. (Hugh O'Connor, amateur psychologist!) I had two options, I figured: take it easy or stop seeing her. It seemed worth trying the first one first.

We went out quite a lot in the next couple of weeks, mostly with the twins, but sometimes, in the evenings, on our own.

We went to films at the *Irish Film Centre* or the *Lighthouse* (which was fine by me), to a scientific lecture in the RDS (amazingly, it was less than terminally boring) and even to a concert in the National Concert Hall. (What else did I learn this year, Ms Blenchley? I got me a bit of culture – you ought to be pleased.) At times I thought I was making progress – and then it was back to square one. And the worst of it was that I could never understand *why*. I mean, Rachel liked holding hands, hugging (or, more accurately, *being* hugged), even kissing (as long as it wasn't too intense). But it was a bit like going out with Cinderella: as soon as we got to her front door, she turned into an ice maiden and I felt like a pumpkin.

Did she care at all? I knew how *I* felt about *her*: I couldn't get her out of my mind, couldn't wait to see her, went all funny inside whenever I touched her. Sometimes I thought she felt the same way about me; other times, I could have been her brother or the pizza delivery boy. It was driving me up the wall.

"How are you getting on with Marie-Claire?" I asked Dave (ie *Is Rachel's behaviour normal?*).

Dave rolled his eyes. "Great! Fab! Wow!"

Um. Yes. What did that tell me? That Dave and Marie-Claire were snogging round the clock? Or that Dave hadn't got any further than I had, but wasn't going to admit it?

As for the school newspaper, *The Door*, if you think it was running smoothly all this time, you're wrong.

Nobody had come down on us for the comic strip yet, but it was only a matter of time. The trouble was a new character that Rachel and Kate had brought on to the staff of Swiss Valley High: an art teacher whom they'd named, yes, I know, Laurence Van Rubens. Suzie and her friends were now calling him Lecherous Larry because of the way he leched after the attractive girls.

It was obvious (to all of *us*, anyway) that the gorgeous Suzie, her of the long blonde hair and even longer legs, was a thinly-disguised feminist version of Marie-Claire. And that, had the strip been in colour (which, thank God, we couldn't afford), Lecherous Larry would have had carroty red hair and been nicknamed Creepy Chris instead. Kate's artwork was excellent: he had a foxy face, shifty eyes and a mouth permanently drawn up in a leer. Gleeson might be a nerd, I remember thinking, but Lecherous Larry of Swiss Valley High looked set to become an out-and-out psychopath.

People were talking about it right through the school. I'd even overheard a couple of sixth-year prefects complaining in the yard one day. "That cartoon strip in the Transition Year newspaper should be banned," said one of them. "Yeah," agreed the other. "It's getting so's you can't even chat up a girl without someone accusing you of harassment."

I warned Rachel that she was heading for trouble but she brushed off my warnings. "It's just romantic slush for girls," she told me. "If anyone wants to read anything else into it, that's their problem."

So *Swiss Valley High* was a time bomb waiting for someone, probably Mr Franklin, to set it off. But the paper could just as easily self-combust, due to the rifts which were starting to show between Rachel's hardline morality and the less PC attitudes of the rest of us.

And it wasn't just what got into the letters page or the *Ask Mabel* column that we argued about. Brian was regularly indignant that so many of his jokes were scrapped. "They're sexist," Rachel would say shortly. Or, "They're racist." "They're *funny*," Brian would insist. "Just because *you* have no sense of humour, what gives you the right to dictate what other people should laugh at?" And some of Kerry's articles on dieting and skin care got thrown out too: they were demeaning to women or involved the exploitation of animals.

Dave, of course, went out of his way to wind her up: he wrote articles supporting nuclear energy, banks, the meat industry, even the tobacco industry, all well-researched (Dave learnt a lot this year too, Ms Blenchley!) and pretty persuasive. He ought to become a lawyer, Dave, when he grows up. (If he ever does.)

He also started a campaign to *Bring Back Real Men.* "Like *Real Ale*," he explained. "You must admit it's about time. I mean, look at all these books we're supposed to read, especially the ones written by women: have you ever noticed that all the mothers are sorting out the planet or learning self-assertiveness or being astrophysicists or mending the car, while the men are wimpy rugs for them to walk on? Count me the number of fathers in books who are completely impractical dweebs who can't even boil an egg – or else, who can do nothing else. That is, when fathers are allowed to exist at all."

He had a point, I must admit. And Rachel had to let him have his say in the paper. If she didn't, he accused her of intolerance. As this was the one thing she hated most, she hadn't a leg to stand on.

The *Real Men* campaign wasn't the only campaign in the paper that Rachel had trouble with. Some weeks before, we'd held a referendum, on Marie-Claire's suggestion, to decide what to do with the profits from the paper. Yes, we were actually making a profit! It didn't come to much, but the subject managed to cause a lot of aggro, especially as Brian and Dave felt we should keep it for ourselves and the girls wanted to give it to charity.

Very few readers had bothered to reply. Once we'd weeded out those who'd done so for a joke (most of them had named themselves as worthy causes and the rest had shown imagination that would have fascinated Freud), we'd been left with a pile of letters from first years demanding that the money went to a donkey sanctuary. There had been a programme on children's TV, apparently, full of pictures of sad geriatric donkeys, and most of first year had seen it.

Rachel had wanted to give a donation to an inner-city charity for deprived kids. Marie-Claire had gone for famine-relief in Africa. Kerry had supported Marie-Claire. Brian hadn't said much. Louise, predictably, had wanted new equipment for the school PE department while Kate would have liked more materials for the art room. Dave had made a case for the Pro-Life Society, just to wind Rachel up. (She'd fallen for it.) Like him, I didn't really care where the money went (as I said, there wasn't that much of it anyway), though I'd supported Rachel, of course.

"The donkeys have it," Dave had announced after we'd all had our say. "The rest of you are outnumbered."

"Nobody will know," Marie-Claire had argued. "And people are more important than donkeys."

Rachel had been forced to side with Dave. "Sorry, Marie-Claire. You're right. But we have to stick with the majority decision and all these kids do want it to go to donkeys, so donkeys it'll have to be."

Now Frankenstein asked us to hold another referendum. He must have been keeping an eye on the paper, although so far he didn't appear to have noticed what was going on in *Swiss Valley High.*

He obviously hoped, like Rachel, to use *The Door* to further his own causes. And the cause he was rooting for at that moment was school uniform.

Every so often, someone (parents, teachers, even pupils)

thinks it would be a great idea to introduce a uniform into our school. Make us all neat and tidy. (Though if whoever believes that has ever stood at the gates of a school when the inmates come flooding out and actually *looked* at the way their uniform is worn, they'd most likely change their minds.)

Fortunately, up till now, the idea had never got any further. But it must have been in the air again, as Franklin suggested we ran a second referendum "to ascertain the wishes of the school" in this regard.

"He'll just ignore our wishes anyway," Brian muttered. "He's a headmaster."

"We'll have to do it, though," Marie-Claire said. "He's insisting."

So we did.

Slightly more people wrote in this time around, but it was still only a tiny fraction of the pupils in the school. And, amazingly, most of them wanted a uniform.

"They must be mad," Dave groaned when we'd counted out the result. "What's wrong with jeans?"

"I can see their point," Marie-Claire said. "At least you wouldn't have to wonder what to put on in the morning. And everyone would be wearing the same: you wouldn't have some people showing off in designer clothes."

"That bothers you, does it?" I asked.

"No . . . o. But it could bother some people."

"The trouble is," Rachel pointed out, "if we print this as a percentage, it looks as if over 60% of the school wants a uniform. And yet not much more than 5% of the total pupils responded to the question. So only 60% of 5% want a uniform, which is about 3%. And Franklin will use our results to push a uniform through."

"You're assuming the other 95% *don't* want a uniform. Maybe they do." Dave was stirring it, as usual.

"The point is, we don't know. And if we print this poll, it looks as if we do."

"All opinion polls are like that," Kate said. "Nobody should ever judge anything by them."

"Yes, I *know*. But people do judge by them. And Franklin certainly will. Do we want to be responsible for bringing a uniform into the school?" Rachel sounded really worried.

"OK," I said. "So we've got three choices: we don't print anything (and then Frankenstein's going to want to know why), we print the results as we have them, or we fake it and say that a majority voted against a uniform."

"Or we could say that less than 5% of the school voted to introduce a uniform, which would be true enough," Rachel suggested.

"The truth, but not the whole truth and certainly not nothing but the truth," Dave mocked. "Shame on you, Rachel. Where are your principles? What happened to 'publish and be damned'? Not to mention 'opening a door'?

Rachel looked embarrassed. I put a motion to the floor (I love that expression: as if the floorboards could talk back) that we announced that too few people voted to give a proper result. Marie-Claire wasn't too happy, but only Dave objected outright.

"Carried," I announced.

What else did we learn this year? That principles are fine, but sticking to them isn't always as easy as you think.

Chapter 20

Companion. A gender-inclusive nonheterosexist substitute for "boyfriend," "wife," "husband," or "spouse." But because it is also a nonspeciesist substitute for "pet" or "animal friend," extreme care should be taken before using it.

The *Official Politically Correct Dictionary and Handbook,* Beard & Cerf, HarperCollins

Easter was great. I saw a lot of Rachel over the holidays and we even managed to get rid of the twins on a regular basis: Josie and Pete had broken up (a 'temporary cooling-off period', Josie called it, I don't know what Pete referred to it as), so at last Josie was starting to do her fair share of baby-sitting.

Even though we were a couple now, Rachel never invited me into her house. She'd been to mine, met Ma, Da and the cat, and everybody had been polite and friendly. Even the cat. I told myself that there had to be a perfectly good reason why she kept me strictly to the far side of the front door. And it wasn't as if I was that desperate to meet her dad or get to know Josie better: I saw enough of teachers at school, after all, and big sisters have never done much for me.

We found plenty to do outside the house. Rachel dragged

me hillwalking, for a start. We talked as we ploughed across bogs and up perpendicular mountains in howling winds and horizontal rain. And no, we didn't just debate famine in Africa or homelessness on Dublin streets or cruelty to animals. Rachel wasn't *always* into political correctness, never mind what Dave said. We discussed music, school, life, death, the universe – you know, the usual. And she wasn't above gossiping about Josie and Pete or telling me far-out stories about the twins and about Mrs Gillespie who minded them after school (and who must have had nerves of steel or be in real danger of being carted off to the funny farm. Shit, there I go being socially inconsiderate again. Sorry, Rache). She even spoke about her mother, about the accident, and about how much she's missed her since.

The one thing she never *ever* mentioned was her dad.

I did ask her, once, after I'd bumped into Marie-Claire in Dún Laoghaire and she'd had a go at me, yet again, to try and find out more. "How's your father coping without your mother?" I murmured casually as we sat drinking coffee in my kitchen one evening.

"He's all right. Let's not talk about him." And she turned the conversation to something else.

Unfortunately, her father wasn't the only subject which she fenced around with barbed wire and huge signs: DANGER – KEEP OUT!

She played me like a yo-yo, emotionally. I didn't think, even then, that she really knew what she was doing to me, but it was still pretty hard to take. I mean, there were times when she was affectionate, snuggled up to me, seemed to want to be kissed and cuddled. But there was some invisible line beyond which I could not get.

"What *do* you want, Rache?" I asked, one day when we were up in the hills. The sun was actually shining for a change, the hills were gleaming, the streams burbling, the lambs baaing and spring was in the air. I'd been feeling amorous – and Rachel had given me the red light yet again.

She didn't answer immediately. Then, "Don't try to rush me, Hugh. I like you, I like going out with you. But there's too much . . . I just don't have *time* to get really involved – with you or anyone else." She turned her green eyes on me. "If you can't handle that, OK. I'll understand. But don't expect me to *pretend* just to please you."

No. No one would expect Rachel Cross to pretend *anything* to please *anyone*.

Why did I put up with it? I can hear you asking. There must have been easier girls to cuddle out there.

I'm sure there were, though I hadn't found one myself. And I didn't want another girl, I wanted Rachel. So I decided to play it her way, take it slowly, see how things went.

Of course I didn't tell Dave any of this. I knew what his reaction would have been: he'd have set up a book on "How long will it take Hugh O'Connor to thaw ice maiden Rachel Cross and has he a hope in hell?" and taken bets. Some days, I felt the odds were stacked in my favour. Other days, it was a thousand to one against.

But I didn't give up. In a way, it was like a challenge. I'd got close enough to Rachel when her defences were down to know that she was the opposite of an iron hand in a velvet glove. In her, the outside was hard but the inside soft as toasted marshmallow. One day she was going to trust me and I'd find out what it was that had made her build this hard shell around herself. She would look at me and, suddenly, all barriers would be down between us.

Well, Ma's soppy magazines had to get it right some time, didn't they?

Chapter 21

Parents are the last people on earth who ought to have children.

Samuel Butler 1835-1902

We were a couple of weeks into the summer term when one of the pieces in the puzzle that was Rachel fell into place. I was coming home from school on the bus, minding my own business, thinking of this and that, when gradually the conversation in the seat behind me started filtering into my ears. Two young lads were talking.

"Cross, Crosser, Crossest," said one with a giggle.

"Most hugely, ginormously, incredibly, mega Cross," said the other. "I wouldn't be surprised if they chucked him out."

"Nah. You can't get rid of teachers. Everyone knows that."

"Yeah, but Cross really went ape. I mean violent, man. You should've seen him. We thought Keith was done for. Cross picked him up like he was a rabbit and shook him so hard his head nearly came off. You should've heard his language! I mean, they go on about *us* swearing – they should listen to Cross! And all because Keith flicked some slime at the ceiling and it fell on Cross's head."

The second boy laughed. "On his bald patch?"

"Yeah. Classic, it was. But he really went for Keith afterwards."

"You can't blame him, though."

"Nah, he went right over the top. I mean, it was like he was on drugs or something."

"Maybe he was? Cross a druggie! What happened then?"

"Dunno. He sort of snapped out of it. He dropped Keith like he was red-hot or something, told us to copy out the page we were at and left the room. Never came back. We had a real party till the bell went."

"Mega," said the second boy. "D'you think Keith's parents'll take him to court? Grievous bodily harm or something?"

"Wouldn't be surprised," said the first. "I'd get my parents to sue the school for half a million if he ever tried that shit on me."

"Hey, we're here. Come on."

They legged it down the stairs and I watched as they spilled out on to the pavement: two lads from St Malachy's by their uniform.

Rachel's dad was a teacher. Did he teach at St Malachy's? I tried to convince myself they'd been talking about another teacher called Cross. It wasn't that unusual a name. But somehow, I knew it was Rachel's dad. What had they said? He'd gone ape. Lost his temper completely. Just about assaulted a pupil.

Teachers did that all the time, though. Well, maybe not as much as those kids had been going on about. Was Rachel's dad losing it? Was the strain getting too much for him? What strain? The strain of being a widower? *Or the strain of facing up to whatever he was doing to his children?*

I shook my head to get rid of that last thought. If I didn't watch it, I'd soon be as bad as Marie-Claire.

Still, the suspicion was there, had been there for weeks only I hadn't admitted it, and it wouldn't go away.

When in doubt, ask your Mammy. It had worked when I was five, it was maybe worth a try now. I got off at my stop and walked home.

Ma was back before me. She heard me come in.

"That you, Hugh?"

A stupid question. Who else was it likely to be?

I stuck my head in the door. "Hi!" She was sitting on the floor, mending a rip in the sofa: just the picture of domesticity, competence and reliability I needed right then.

"You're back early. Don't tell me you came straight home from school for a change."

"No, I went via Outer Mongolia, but it was one of the new, fast buses."

"Ha, ha," she answered on cue. That's the essence of a good parent-child relationship, predictability. "Outer Mongolia I could buy, but not a fast Dublin bus."

"Ma?"

"Yes?"

"What would you do if you thought someone was being abused?"

She took a pin out of her mouth and looked at me seriously. What I like about Ma is that she knows when you're messing and when you're not. She didn't make a fuss and ask me what I was on about, just took it calmly, as if I'd asked her for a recipe for lasagne or what was the capital of Zimbabwe. "What kind of abuse?"

How many kinds were there? "You know what I mean. Fathers . . ." I felt myself getting hot but carried on all the same, "with . . . with their children."

She thought for a moment. "I'd try to get them to talk

about it, I suppose. Try to persuade them to go for help. Why? Do you know someone who's being abused like that?"

"I'm not sure. Maybe."

"Do you want to tell me about it?"

I was tempted. After all, Ma had met Rachel, they had got on together OK the couple of times she'd been to the house, and Ma *was* a social worker. But I still wanted to believe I was imagining things. I couldn't be *sure* that Mr Cross was . . . was . . . No! The whole idea was way out of line. And, anyway, if I *did* say something, even just to Ma, just to get her to tell me how silly I was being . . . she wouldn't just leave it there. All sorts of wheels would start to turn. And if Marie-Claire was wrong – she *had* to be wrong – I wouldn't only be left looking a right nerd, but Rachel would definitely never talk to me ever again.

"It's OK," I told Ma. "Forget it."

"Is it one of your friends from school?" I didn't answer, but she went on anyway, "Maybe you could persuade them to see Mr Whatsits, your guidance counsellor?"

The thought of Rachel baring her soul to Mr Hayward almost made me smile. A pig would fly first. "It's OK, Ma. Leave it."

"Talk to whoever it is anyway, Hugh. If they *are* being abused, even talking to a friend would help. And let me know if there's anything I can do. If this *is* an abuse situation, you can't just leave it, you know. He – or she?" she looked at me really closely, I gave nothing back, "has to get help. And it's not something you can carry on your own shoulders, love. You must realize that."

"It's OK. Thanks. I have to go out now."

She bit her lip, seemed about to say something and then smiled. "Fine. You know when tea is – ring me if you're going to be late. And, Hughie, if this *is* abuse, your friend needs help. And you may need help to talk about it too. Remember I'm here and I'll do anything I can. Just ask."

"Thanks, Ma," I said again. "Oh, and one other thing. Would you say you're a feminist?"

"Yes."

"Oh. Right, that's that then. See you." I made for the door.

Ma gave me a worried look. "As long as you're sure that's that," she said. "Bye, love. Good luck."

It was a Thursday, the day Rachel and Marie-Claire had a free period at the end of the afternoon and so got out earlier than me and Dave. Rachel would be home now. I'd go round and see her and *force* her to talk about her dad. There wasn't any dark terrible secret in her life – all I needed was for her to tell me so.

I pressed her bell and listened to it ring inside the house. I waited for footsteps. All I heard was raised voices, but I couldn't make out what was being said.

I hit the bell again and knocked on the door for good measure. Still no answer. All my doubts came flooding back. *What was going on?*

I looked at the neighbouring houses. Should I try banging on one of their doors? "Excuse me, but I think Rachel Cross might be in trouble. Will you call the police?" No, perhaps not. Not yet, anyway.

I rang again. This time I heard footsteps come down the stairs, someone fumbled with a chain, and finally the door was opened a crack.

Alice looked out at me. She was wearing pyjamas with pink flying horses on them and was clutching a teddy bear tightly. She looked as if she'd been crying.

"Hi, Alice." I made an effort to sound normal and cheerful. "It's Hugh. Can I come in and talk to Rachel?"

Alice hesitated. Through the gap in the door I saw Rachel

come down the stairs. She put an arm round Alice and gave her a hug. "Go back to bed," she whispered. "I'll be up in a minute to tuck you in."

Bed? It was hardly more than five o'clock.

She started to shut the door.

"Hey, Rache! Wait a minute! I only want to talk!"

"I'm just taking off the chain." Sure enough, the door opened again and Rachel stood in the shadows of the hall looking out at me. "What on earth are you doing here?"

It was like old times. As if we'd never gone out together. "I came round to see if . . . if . . ." I babbled. My imagination was working overtime. I tried to see if she'd been bruised but her hair was loose and hung over her face. And the hall, as I said, was pretty dark. "Are you all right?" I asked.

"I'm fine." She glanced upstairs, then turned back to me. "Sorry, Hugh, but I can't come out just now. I'll see you some other time. OK?"

She started to close the door.

"Wait a minute!" I said quickly, jamming my foot in the door like a travelling salesman – and learning why travelling salesmen wear hard shoes and not runners. "What about later? After dinner?"

"Later? I don't know. Probably not. I'm sorry, but I have to go now." And the door shut in my face.

I rang the bell again. Nothing happened.

Well, what would you have done? I turned away and walked home. I won't deny that I was angry. I'd been going out with Rachel for weeks now, we'd shared our most intimate thoughts (well, some of them anyway), she acted as if she was fond of me (even if she'd never actually said she loved me), and here I was, back at square one, having the door slammed in my face – again.

Forget her, I said to myself. Stop worrying about her. I had been adding two and two together to make forty and it was all because of Marie-Claire. She had an over-active imagination and read too many books. She didn't realise that books were dangerous. If she'd stuck to computer games, she wouldn't have this trouble confusing fact and fantasy. And Rachel was as bad: a control freak who didn't care about anyone except herself.

Women! I'd had enough of them. That was it. I'd forget the whole lot of them and get on with my life.

But then I remembered how worried Rachel had looked. And how Alice had been crying. *I couldn't just walk away from them.*

It's a problem I've got: I'll always rescue stray dogs, even if they bite me. I decided to talk to Rachel at school the next day and this time, I'd *demand* a straight answer.

But something happened the next day which put all thoughts of Rachel's family life right out of my head.

Chapter 22

When the *New York World* satirized Lincoln in 1863, the paper was shut down and its editors arrested on Lincoln's personal orders.

I didn't manage to get Rachel on her own until after break. Nobody would have guessed that she'd actually slammed the door in my face less than twenty-four hours earlier – she seemed delighted to see me and immediately started on about some problem with the newspaper, the ultra-efficient editor again. It was really weird, almost as if she was two people. One, the one we saw at school, was up-front, decisive, and on top of things. The other, the "home" Rachel, was secretive, emotional and pretty manipulative. I wished I knew why.

We were walking along the mall. I was still determined to have it out with her and was trying various conversations in my head. I thought of repeating what I'd heard the two kids say on the bus, of making it into a joke ("You know, I actually wondered for a moment if they were talking about your father!") – and then Gleeson stopped us.

"Come with me, you two." He turned and marched off towards the English room.

We looked at each other and followed him.

"Sit down." He pointed to the desks in the front row.

We sat. Teachers aren't stupid: they know that if you're sitting and they're standing, you're at a disadvantage.

Going over to the window, he stared out into the yard for a moment, ran his fingers through his mop of ginger hair (it needed a cut, I noticed) and then turned to face us.

"OK, then. Tell me why you're hounding me in this newspaper of yours."

I caught myself looking like a stranded fish and closed my mouth. Rachel didn't even ask what he was talking about; she went straight for the jugular. "What makes you think it's you?"

"Ah, come on now. It's obvious."

She continued to attack, like one of these Rottweiler lawyers on the telly: "Are you saying you can see a resemblance to yourself in the *Swiss Valley High* cartoon?"

Couldn't everyone? Every thinking person in the school ought to have sussed it out by now. Over the weeks, Lecherous Larry had gradually begun to look more and more like Creepy Chris. Rachel and Kate were even using situations Gleeson was famous for, eying girls in class, touching them "accidentally", that sort of thing. Only the week before, there'd been a scene at a school dance where Larry had cut in on Suzie and her boyfriend and had had his hands all over her. It was a miracle that Gleeson had taken so long to see it. Certainly most of the pupils in Monkscross assumed that Lecherous Lar was meant to be him and were waiting, like crowds outside the house of a mass-murderer, to see what he was going to do about it. Now I knew.

"I am asking why you feel justified in attacking me like this."

"The cartoon is a work of fiction." Rachel reserved her defence. "You're welcome to read what you want into it. I'll say this, though: if we *had* intended Lecherous Larry to be you (which I'm not admitting we did), you ought to know why."

Gleeson sighed. "What's eating you, Rachel? You're an intelligent girl. And you are going around publicly accusing me of sexual harassment, practically rape. You can't do that."

"If the cap fits . . . "

"Rachel! I'm a married man. If I wanted a woman, I wouldn't go for schoolkids."

"No? Then why do you ogle all the girls in class? Why make all the smutty jokes?"

"So that's it. You can't take a joke. I didn't realise you were such a prude, Rachel."

She didn't lose her cool. I admired her (even if I was doing nothing to back her up). "The way you talk about things is not a joke. Maybe the boys laugh, but the girls don't. Or haven't you noticed?"

"Some girls have no sense of humour. Hugh here will agree with that, won't you, Hugh?"

He winked at me. I scowled back at him.

"And," he went on, "if you don't want to be 'ogled', as you put it, why do you all wear such short skirts and leave the top of your blouses unbuttoned? Women enjoy a bit of attention. It's flattering."

"So we ask for it and you do it just to make us little women feel good?" The sarcasm in Rachel's voice would have stripped paint at fifty yards.

Gleeson sighed. "I brought you in here to warn you, Rachel. If you go any further with this, I shall fight back. So I suggest you wind up *Sweet Valley School,* or whatever you call your petty little cartoon, *now*, or you may find that not only your newspaper will be wound up, but your career at Monkscross as well. Do I make myself clear?"

"Extremely."

"Then think carefully, my girl." He appealed to me again. "Hugh, can you not make her see reason? Try to put some sense into her thick head before she gets into *real* trouble." He went over to open the door. "There's the bell, now. Off with you both. And don't let me hear another word about this nonsense."

Rachel stalked out and I scurried after her.

I expected her to turn on me, to ask me why I hadn't backed her up, but Rachel was always a one-man (one-woman) show: she had met Gleeson's first attack; her mind was already on the next stage of the battle.

"Get everyone together for a meeting today after school," she ordered. "Tell them it's urgent."

I was tempted to snap to attention and throw a salute. I didn't, though. I told myself that there were probably sides to me that Rachel didn't like either and that nobody was perfect. And she was right: we needed an editorial meeting to decide what to do.

"OK," I agreed.

We met after school, Rachel, Marie-Claire, Kerry, Brian, Dave and me. Kate had a music lesson and wasn't going to cancel it. Louise had a hockey match. Brian hadn't wanted to be there at all and had told me what to do with myself when I'd put it to him, but Kerry had dragged him along. As for Dave, he'd come for the laugh, he told me.

He got his boot in right at the start of the meeting. Rachel explained how Gleeson was out to muzzle *Swiss Valley High* and had threatened to close down the newspaper. "It's pure censorship," she said. "We can't give in."

"Before we start discussing that," Dave sounded suspiciously innocent, "I'd be grateful if you'd answer a point of information, Rache. It's been bothering me for some time, now. Why, if you're all for saving the whale and outlawing fox-hunting, do you and Kate want to drive poor Mr Gleeson out of teaching?"

I hid a smile.

Surprisingly, Kerry, of all people, dealt with him before Rachel could erupt. "*Poor* Mr Gleeson? Have you lost your marbles, Dave? Everyone knows he's a sexist pervert with a sewer for a mind." I had never heard her this upset; even when Dave slagged her fashion pieces, she usually just grinned (although Dave claimed that this was only because she was so thick she couldn't see his sarcasm). Gleeson must have touched a nerve, if not more, with her too.

"He's not that bad," Brian remarked. "OK, so he makes the odd stupid joke. But don't we all?"

"I agree with Kerry," Marie-Claire said quickly, before Rachel could floor Brian with a few home truths. "Mr Gleeson can be dreadfully embarrassing. But," she went on, "he has a point, Rachel. You and Kate have gone too far with the *Swiss Valley High* strip. It's not funny any more. I think you should get rid of Lecherous Larry and bring it back to the *Chalet-School*-type stories you started with."

"It was never meant to be funny. And it was certainly never meant to be just an Enid Blyton spin-off."

"The *Chalet School* books aren't by Enid Blyton," Marie-Claire informed us helpfully.

"It was meant to prove a point," Rachel insisted, ignoring her. "We can't let Gleeson win."

"It has certainly proved a point," Dave commented. "The point that you and Kate are paranoid."

"You don't have to be paranoid to object to sexual harassment."

"Marie-Claire's right," I put in. "That comic strip has run for long enough. It's time to chuck it and get a new one in."

"Maybe," Rachel said, conceding ground for the first time.

Strike when the iron is hot: one of Ma's favourite mottoes. (It's worrying how you find yourself quoting your mother sometimes.) "OK, then," I said firmly. "So we've decided to wrap up Lecherous Larry. Can you and Kate bring the cartoon to an end for next week's edition?"

"There's a lot of people follow *Swiss Valley High*," Brian objected. "It's one of the things people buy the paper for."

"Yeah, I know. But Rachel and Kate can come up with another storyline. One that won't have the teachers getting their knickers in a twist."

"Do you think Gleeson wears knickers?" Dave asked thoughtfully.

"Shut up, you," I told him. "Well?" I asked Rachel.

"I suppose so. It seems a shame, though. Just when we were getting the strip exactly where we wanted it."

I didn't at all like the look in her eye. Gleeson had obviously copped on just in time: if Rachel had something worse in store for him than the cartoons she and Kate had already written, then we were talking major libel here. "Promise me you won't do anything stupid, Rache," I begged her.

She grinned, reminding me of the Cheshire cat in *Alice.* "Would I?"

Marie-Claire, Kerry and myself all turned on her at the same time.

"OK, OK. I'll be good. Next week's strip will end on a

happy note of reconciliation and Lecherous Lar will see the light and change from a perv to a New Man, just to keep you all happy."

There was still that look in her eye. Could we trust her?

"I just hope Gleeson's learnt his lesson," said Marie-Claire.

I hoped Rachel had learnt hers.

Chapter 23

> Three hundred and fourteen acres of trees are used to make the newsprint for the average Sunday edition of *The New York Times.* There are nearly 63,000 trees in 314 acres.

We walked down to the bus stop together, the four of us.

"There's a gig at the *Purty Kitchen* tonight," Dave said. "Anyone interested?"

"Who's playing?" Marie-Claire asked.

"The Green Sausage Machine." He saw her face. "Come on, you'll like them."

"What d'you two think?" She looked at Rachel and me.

"Rache?"

"Count me out."

"We could do something else," I said.

"I can't. I'm . . . busy this evening." She frowned. "Come on, bus," she muttered impatiently.

"Are you picking up the twins?" I asked.

"No. It's Josie's day off."

"What's your hurry, then? We could go into Dún Laoghaire for a coffee or something."

"Sorry, Hugh. I didn't realize I'd be so late and I didn't warn anyone. I've got to get home."

What *was* it with her? She'd been fine all day at school and now, all of a sudden, we were back to the cold-shoulder treatment. And again, the change came as soon as she thought of home.

Have you ever seen that film *Gone with the Wind* where Vivienne Leigh blows hot and cold with Clark Gable and he walks off at the end? Before I had time to work out whether I gave a damn or not, her bus arrived and whisked her away. Rachel the witch going back to brew more anti-Gleeson spells – or Rachel the victim, returning to whatever was going on in the Cross family home? I wished I knew.

Marie-Claire must have been thinking the same thing. "Have you tried asking Rachel what's wrong, Hugh?"

"Why are you sure something is?" Defensive wasn't in it.

"I *know* something is. Have you *still* not met her dad?"

I hadn't met her dad. And I hadn't told anyone about what I'd overheard on the bus, either.

"Give it a rest, Marie-Claire," Dave advised. "You're obsessed with Rachel. She's a big girl now. She's well able to look after herself."

"I don't know. I worry about her."

So did I. And I didn't know either.

Dave grinned at me. "Cheer up, Hugh. The course of true love never did run smooth. With exceptions, of course." He gave Marie-Claire a hug. "So why don't you forget Superwoman and come down to the *Purty* this evening with us losers? One night's slumming won't kill you."

"I wish you'd stop going on about Rachel feeling superior to the rest of us," I muttered automatically, but my heart wasn't in it. It would be a good idea to go out with less complicated company. A night listening to a band sad enough to call itself *The Green Sausage Machine* might be just what I needed.

It worked, too. I spent the whole evening not even thinking of Rachel and fell asleep the moment my head hit the pillow.

That was Friday.

Marie-Claire phoned the next morning. "Hugh? Do you think we ought to get help for Rachel?"

She'd got me out of bed. I'd like to say that I hadn't been thinking *anything*, least of all about Rachel, but she was like a thorn under my skin: no matter how hard I tried to shove her out of my mind, she kept seeping back in round the edges. (Sorry about the mixed metaphor, but you know what I mean.)

"Why don't you ring her, Hugh? Just to see how she is."

"Why don't you? You're her friend."

"She won't tell me anything. You're closer to her than I am – she'll talk to you."

I could have told Marie-Claire the truth: that I was about as close to Rachel, at that moment, as Australia is to Dalkey Hill. I didn't, though – we men have our pride.

And it was either pride or stupidity (all right, *and* concern – can I help it if I'm a wimp?), but I picked up the phone and dialled Rachel's number.

One of the twins answered. "Hello?"

"Hi. Is that Alice or Conor?"

"Conor."

"Is Rachel there?"

"Rachel's with Daddy."

Rachel's with Daddy: what did that mean? "Can you tell her Hugh's on the phone?"

"OK." The voice sounded very small and unhappy.

I waited, drumming my fingers on the phone shelf.

"Hugh? How's things?" I don't know what I'd expected but I was surprised when Rachel answered so normally.

"Fine. Are you OK?"

"Yeah. Why shouldn't I be?"

We seemed to be having this conversation a lot lately. I moved on to the next gambit, Knight to Queen Two: "How's your dad?"

For once the Queen didn't rush to his defence. "Not great," she said.

Watch it, I warned myself. She's finally admitted that something's wrong: whatever you do now, make sure you say the right thing. (Come back, Ma, all is forgiven!)

"Is he sick?" I asked. No, that could mean a couple of things. "Have you called the doctor?" That seemed safe enough.

"Daddy doesn't want to see him. I wish he would. He needs . . ." She broke off. "It's in the kitchen, Conor. Sorry, Hugh. I'll have to go. Thanks for calling."

"What about later? Can you come out?" (I *know*: "Here he goes again . . ." you're saying. Just get off my case, will you?)

She hesitated. "I wish I could, Hugh. I'd really love to see you." (*There, now!* That's a bit more like it!) "But I'd better not. I'm needed here. See you in school next week." She even added, "Have a good weekend." As if that made everything all right.

I threw a cushion at the cat. This was doing my head in.

I tried to forget about her all weekend, but when I met her in the canteen on Monday, she had black circles under her eyes and looked so tired I started feeling all protective again.

"Are you OK?" I even put my arm round her. I wasn't really surprised when she didn't seem to mind, like there was nothing wrong between us: Jekyll and Hyde again. "You said your father wasn't well at the weekend – is he any better?" I asked carefully.

"He's much the same. He still won't see a doctor."

Honesty again! I went for the jackpot. "What's wrong with him?"

She hesitated. "It's just depression. He's been a bit . . . down . . . since Mummy died."

Depression. So that was it! Have you ever seen one of these black-and-white films with dirty-faced coal miners in poverty-stricken towns surrounded by giant slag heaps? I felt as if a weight as black and heavy as a slag heap had been lifted off me – which proves that Marie-Claire's suspicions had got to me a lot more than I'd want to admit, even to myself. So the only thing wrong in the Cross family was that Mr Cross had depression? Fantastic. Sure, depression can be pretty serious, I knew that. But it was better than . . . the other.

The thought did sidle into my mind that Rachel could still be covering up, but I refused to give it house room. "Depression can be cured," I said encouragingly.

Rachel wasn't listening. "It's not as if it's been easy for any of us," she said, speaking half to herself, "but *we* have to go on with our lives. You can't just stop the world because *you* want to get off."

I put my hand over hers. "You've been great to cope with this all on your own, Rache. But you ought to get help."

She squeezed my hand back. "Thanks, Hugh. I'm fine. I'm Rachel, remember, the one who never cracks up." She smiled but her voice was harsh.

I wanted to kiss her but we were in the canteen. "Come on." I pushed my chair back. "There's still time for a quick walk round the hockey pitch."

She stood up, too. "Sorry, Hugh. I've got things to do. I'm late already."

It was like a slap in the face with a bit of raw liver.

She had "things to do" after school. *And* that evening.

I decided I'd had enough. I washed my hands of her.

I avoided her all Tuesday.

Wednesday was the day we put *The Door* together. I did think of resigning from the paper, but why should I stop doing something I was interested in just because a girl I had once fancied was involved in it too?

It surprised me to find Dave in thc office – he usually left the hard work to the rest of us. "I'm just curious which way Rachel's going to jump with *Swiss Valley High*," he said.

Swiss Valley High? Jesus, I'd almost forgotten. Thinking about it now, I hoped Rachel had seen sense and finished the strip as she'd promised. Life was hard enough without having Frankenstein on my back and the chance of expulsion in the offing.

Kerry and Marie-Claire had got there before us. The pasted-up copy was lying on the table, ready for photocopying, but there was no sign of either Rachel or Kate. And, more worryingly, there was only one pasted-up sheet, the middle spread. The outside spread, which formed the front and back pages, was missing. And the *Swiss Valley High* cartoon was always on the inside of the back page.

Something was rotten in the state of Monkscross, that was for sure.

"I smell a rat," Dave announced.

I looked at him. "What do you suggest we do?"

"Set a trap? Lay down rat poison? Call in the Pied Piper of Hamelin?"

"You know what I mean."

"We'll just have to copy what's here," Kerry suggested. "There must have been some problem with the first sheet. Rachel and Kate are probably sorting it out now. If we get this one photocopied, it won't take long to do the other and put them together."

"How innocent are the minds of those who walk the highways of fashion," Dave remarked to nobody in particular.

Kerry glanced at him suspiciously. "What's he on about?" she asked Marie-Claire.

Dave smiled. "Do you want us to spell it out for you?"

"If you're going to be insulting . . ."

"I think they're talking about the *Swiss Valley High* strip," Marie-Claire explained. "You remember, Rachel and Kate are supposed to be winding it up this week."

"And are probably winding up Gleeson instead," Dave put in. "If not stitching him up completely – a metaphor which should appeal to Kerry here as our esteemed fashion editor."

"Be serious," Marie-Claire told him. "We have to decide what to do."

"I still don't see . . ."

I sighed. "Listen, Kerry. If Rachel and Kate print a nice happy end to this particular series of *Swiss Valley High,* tying it up in a pretty pink bow and letting Lecherous Larry off the hook, we're fine: the paper comes out tomorrow, the punters buy it, nobody has a fit and everyone's delighted. But if they decide to end with a bang . . ."

"Surely not," Dave interrupted. "No sex in *The Door,* please; remember we sell to children."

I ignored him. "Look, Rachel's made sure we can't see the last strip because it isn't here, so I'd say she and Kate are planning on a really big finale. So, do we help them along by photocopying the rest of the paper, all ready for them to add the first and last pages tomorrow? Or do we trash the whole thing now? That is the question."

"But my article's in there," Kerry squealed. "I put a lot of work into that."

"As did we all," Dave agreed. "So?" he looked at me.

"I think we should trash it."

"Hugh's right. If Rachel and Kate are going to get into trouble, it's up to us to stop them." That was Marie-Claire.

"What about 'Publish and be damned'? Our Rache's favourite motto?"

"Are *you* willing to be damned?"

He didn't answer.

We stood around looking thoughtful for a minute. Then, "What could they do to us?" Kerry asked. "I mean, *Swiss Valley High*'s just Rachel and Kate. The rest of us aren't responsible for it."

"All for one and one for all," Dave quoted. "There's something called collective responsibility – and I have a feeling that's the sort of thing Frankenstein will turn out to believe in."

Kerry dug in her heels. "I think we have a duty to all the other contributors. I mean, it's not just us: there's Brian and Louise and all the people who send in letters and stories and poems."

"She has a point," Dave said. "Not to mention our loyal public, whose day will be *absolutely ruined* if they cannot get this week's edition of *The Door* into their grubby little paws tomorrow."

"I wish I knew what Rachel had up her sleeve," I muttered.

"Her arm?" Dave suggested. "Sorry. It just slipped out."

"Let's get this spread done anyway," Kerry sounded more decisive than I would ever have believed possible. It's amazing how the thought of not being read can change a person. "We can't do any harm photocopying the inside pages. We can always tear them up tomorrow, if necessary."

"You're talking about wasting a dozen rainforests here," I pointed out.

She ignored that.

"Come on, then," Dave said. "Let's live dangerously." He put the pasted-up spread in the photocopier and pressed the button. "Let's strike a blow for freedom of the press."

Chapter 24

> A little sincerity is a dangerous thing, and a great deal of it is absolutely fatal.
>
> Oscar Wilde: *The Critic as Artist*

Rachel and Kate were selling *The Door* in the mall when we got out of class the next lunchtime. Did I come over all weedy when I saw her again? Well, maybe my stomach fluttered a bit – but then I hadn't eaten since breakfast. I could live without Rachel Cross.

The two of them must have come in at the crack of dawn to photocopy the outside pages. And they must have got out of class early to start selling before the rest of us got there. Suspiciouser and suspiciouser, as someone might have said.

I grabbed a copy from Kate and turned to page seven. There at the bottom was the usual *Swiss Valley High* cartoon.

I was conscious of Rachel watching me as I read the strip.

The first frame showed Suzie, white-faced, eyes wide with horror, saying to her friends: "Larry tried to rape me last night!" "Tell Madame!" advises Zena. "She'll never believe Suzie!" says Chantelle.

In frame two, Suzie is standing in Madame's study. "You naughty leetle girl," Madame shouts at her. "How dare you say zees zings about a teacher!"

In frame three, Suzie is packing her bags. "*You* shouldn't have to leave, Sue," Meredith is telling her.

And, in the last frame, Lecherous Larry (looking more like Gleeson than ever) winks at the reader and says: "Women enjoy a bit of attention. It's flattering."

I recognised the quote: Gleeson had said exactly the same to Rachel at our last meeting.

I let out my breath in a whistle.

"Good, isn't it?" Kate asked.

"Are you mad? You said you were going to wind down the strip. Have you both got a death wish or something?"

"We did wind it down," Rachel pointed out. "Suzie is leaving Swiss Valley High. The strip's at an end."

"Which is what all our lives will be after this," I prophesied.

And I wasn't that far wrong.

We were hardly into the first period of the afternoon when a message came round for Dave and myself to go to Mr Franklin's office. Brian, Marie-Claire, Kate, Kerry, Louise and Rachel were there already.

Frankenstein used a different psychological approach to Gleeson: he remained seated in his mock-leather armchair while we all stood (huddled would perhaps be a better word for it) on the carpet in front of him.

I was wrong before: this way, we felt even worse.

Frankenstein leant his elbows on his desk (on which was prominently displayed the latest issue of *The Door*) and steepled his fingers below his chin. He looked at us silently for a full minute. The KGB could have learnt tricks from him.

Then, "All right. Who's going to start?"

We didn't all rush, that was for sure.

"Rachel. I gather you are the prime instigator of this libel."

"What libel, sir?" Rachel was all innocence.

"Don't play games with me. You know what I'm talking about."

"I'm afraid I don't, sir." She sounded genuinely surprised.

Frankenstein was not amused. "I warned you before, Rachel, about this vendetta you seem to be carrying on towards Mr Gleeson."

"I know you did, sir." Butter wouldn't have melted in her mouth. "And I *have* tried to ignore him. Although everyone in the school will back me up about the way he harasses girl pupils."

"He does, sir," Kate cut in. "He's always making smutty remarks and trying to get you to open windows and things so that your skirts ride up and . . ."

"That's enough, Kate," Frankenstein snapped.

"Kate's right," Kerry said firmly. She was full of surprises recently.

"I said that that was enough!"

My turn next. I hadn't been proud of my silence with Gleeson, maybe I could make up for it now. And we had all started the paper with a view to telling the truth. "I agree with the girls, sir. I don't think Mr Gleeson realises what he's saying sometimes," tactful, that, "but I know he upsets some people. And, because he's a teacher, you can't really complain."

Dave cleared his throat. "He uses his position to force attractive girls to dance with him at school discos, even when they don't want to." Dave as well? I hadn't thought he'd have wanted to get involved. But love does strange things to a man – I should know.

Marie-Claire went bright red.

"That is no reason to attack him in this scurrilous manner," Frankenstein told us all. He pointed to the cartoon in *The Door.*

"But what makes you think it's Mr Gleeson, sir?" Rachel asked, even more innocently.

"I am not stupid."

"But it's not him, sir. It's pure fiction. OK," she conceded, "maybe the *idea* for the character came from the way Mr Gleeson abuses his position – or whatever you want to call it. But all the people in the strip are fictitious. It's only a comic strip, after all."

Mr Franklin sat silently looking at us. Apart from Rachel and Kate, both of whom seemed quite unbothered, all of us, even Brian and Louise who hadn't said a word yet, avoided his eye.

Finally he spoke. "Mr Gleeson is a married man," he reminded us. I thought of the day we'd seen him with his six kids at the zoo: you couldn't get more married than that, I agreed. "And a good teacher. However, he has been under some strain recently . . ."

We waited, not daring to look at each other.

"But that is not what we are dealing with here."

I might have guessed: teachers never admit other teachers can be wrong.

"What we have to decide is what to do with the lot of you and with your newspaper. Which, I must admit, has had some good campaigning articles in it and, apart from this unfortunate cartoon, has by and large reflected well on the school."

There was another long pause. I felt that, if I had to look at the pattern in his carpet for much longer, it would become imprinted on my brain.

"I think," Frankenstein finally decided, "that your newspaper should be allowed to continue . . ." we all relaxed, "but only if you, Rachel, as editor, explain to your readers that you are withdrawing this . . . this *Swiss Valley High* cartoon," he wrinkled his nose distastefully as he said it, as if picking up a dirty handkerchief between finger and thumb, "because it is scurrilous and in bad taste. And you will also apologise personally to Mr Gleeson. Do I make myself clear?"

"But I've just told you that the cartoon has nothing to do with Mr Gleeson. How can I apologise for something which doesn't exist?"

Mr Franklin smiled. "I'm sure you will find a way, Rachel. These are my terms: either you retract your insinuations and make sure that this never happens again, or the paper is shut down. It's up to you."

He stood up. The interview was at an end.

Chapter 25

Q. Which fruit sits in the fruit bowl calling for help?
A. A damson in distress.

Q. What's big and hairy and climbs up the Empire State Building in a dress?
A. Queen Kong.

"Thank God that's over," Brian said as we stood in the corridor afterwards. "I don't know about you lot, but as far as I'm concerned, *The Door*'s been well and truly shut. I've had enough, anyway. If you need the odd joke or crossword in future I might be able to come up with something, but otherwise count me out."

Dave raised an eyebrow. "How odd do they have to be? Odder than the ones we've had already?"

Brian made a rude sign at him.

"What about the rest of you?" Rachel asked. "Do you want to stay with the paper or not?"

Dave shrugged. "Brian's got a point. I mean, we've been slogging away at this for three months now. It's time to try something else. I have a band to make famous."

"I think we should keep on with it," Marie-Claire said. "It's fun. And it'll look good on our CVs."

Kerry and Louise agreed with Marie-Claire.

"What about you, Hugh?" Rachel asked. Did she care? Or was I just another possibly defecting worker? Her voice gave nothing away.

"Give the band another try, mate," Dave urged.

I was tempted. I mean, I had sworn off Rachel, hadn't I? Overcome my addiction. If I joined Dave's band, I would hang out with a completely different group – and I might even meet a new woman. Or rather, I might just find the *non*-new woman I had been looking for before, the one who was going to be sweet and adoring (not to mention *predictable*) and love me back.

"I think I'll stick with the newspaper," I heard myself saying. "At least it exists." Sometimes my mouth seems to work on a different wavelength from my brain.

If I'd expected Rachel to jump for joy at this announcement, I was out of luck. Dave's reaction, on the other hand, was suitably over the top. He reeled back, his hand over his heart, pretending to be mortally wounded.

"Of course, that's if Franklin doesn't change his mind and decides to close the whole thing down," I added. "You *are* going to drop the cartoon, aren't you, Rache?"

"Sure," she said. "We'll talk about it on Monday. Usual time, usual place. Anyone who's still interested, be there."

"I suppose we'd better get back to class – there's still half the period left." That was, of course, Marie-Claire.

Rachel hesitated. "You go on," she said. "Tell Miss O'Brien I'm not feeling well and had to go home."

She did look pale, now that I came to think of it. And deathly tired, all of a sudden.

"Are you all right?" Marie-Claire did her mother-hen act again.

"Will people stop asking me if I'm all right!" Rachel snapped. "I'm fine. Just leave me alone!"

She turned and disappeared down the stairs.

There was a time I would have run after her. Now, I let her go.

I had sworn to forget Rachel. And I tried, I really did. But what happened? I worried about her all the rest of that day.

She'd looked really terrible. Had we got it all wrong? Did she have some dread disease that hit her – every now and again – when she didn't have to be Rachel the Capable any more? Or did it all go back to her father, after all?

It wasn't any of my business, I told myself. She'd made that clear enough. And, unlike Marie-Claire, I wasn't going to go rushing in where I wasn't wanted.

I still couldn't get her out of my head, though. By the end of the afternoon, I was a nervous wreck.

Marie-Claire and Dave were going into town after school, so I walked down to the bus stop on my own, still arguing with myself. I definitely wasn't carrying a torch for Rachel any more. No way. On the other hand . . . Well, for a start, she had so few friends. If she really needed help . . . (Rachel, really needing help? Maybe I was coming down with a dread disease myself?)

Her bus came before mine. I got on it. It reached her stop. I got off.

I still hadn't decided what I was going to do when fate took a hand.

"Hugh! Hugh!" It was Conor and Alice. They were trotting along the pavement, tugging Rachel towards me like a couple of overactive huskies.

"Hi, guys," I said back. You can't just ignore six-year-old kids.

"Are you coming home with us?" Alice asked, dropping Rachel's hand and grabbing mine.

"Umm."

"Can you fix my Power Ranger?" Conor flashed a gap-toothed grin up at me. "He's burst."

Why is it so easy to charm little kids and elderly women but so hard to impress girls of my own age? One of life's deeper mysteries, that.

"Please, Rache. *Make* Hugh come home with us."

"Hugh probably has other things to do. He can come another time."

"Please! Please! Please! Please! Please!" Alice and Conor yelled together.

Touching, wasn't it?

We had reached their house. Rachel shrugged. "OK, then," she said to me. "Come in. But just for a minute."

I couldn't believe it: I was finally to cross the Cross threshold! As I followed Alice and Conor up the steps, I didn't know what to expect. Dracula's castle? The witch's gingerbread house? Jack-and-the-beanstalk's giant's lair?

The hall was a normal, slightly scruffy, comfortably untidy hall. The kitchen, which Rachel led us into, a normal very untidy kitchen. No ogre, only Josie sitting at the table reading a magazine.

She looked up as we came in. "You took your time. You've been away for ages."

Rachel helped the kids out of their coats. "Mrs G kept me talking. Her youngest daughter's just got engaged to this fellow in Canada and she wanted to tell me all about the wedding plans."

"Dad's been asking for you. I couldn't calm him down. Will you go in to him now?"

Rachel sighed, seemed to straighten her shoulders and left the kitchen.

"How's your father today?" I asked Josie, as casually as I could.

She didn't answer me directly. "Alice and Conor, why don't you go and watch telly while Hugh and I make the tea?"

The twins scooted out of the kitchen.

Josie plugged in the kettle and then sat down at the table again. "He's getting worse. I don't know how much Rachel's told you . . ." Nothing, I felt like saying, but had the sense not to, ". . . but we're really worried about him. It's been bad for months, he's been impossible to live with, always angry, no matter what we do, criticising all of us for nothing. But now he seems to have given up completely: all he does is get up, sit in a chair in the front room and then go back to bed again. He didn't even go into school the last few days." *Because he'd assaulted a pupil?* I had the sense to keep my theories to myself. "Rachel's the only one who can get him to even eat anything," Josie went on: she didn't seem to share Rachel's discretion, thank goodness. "He's calmer when she's here. I can't do anything with him at all."

"It sounds as if he needs professional help." Hugh O'Connor, your friendly local counsellor, that's me.

"He does. But he's dead against doctors. He thinks they'll just give him pills and he doesn't believe in them. And Rachel keeps hoping he'll pull out of it by himself."

"That's right, tell the world about it." Rachel had come back without us hearing.

Josie looked guilty. "Sorry, Rache. I thought Hugh knew."

The kettle started to boil. Rachel made the tea, put mugs out on the table for the three of us and set a tray for her father. She handed the tray to Josie: "You take this in."

"Well?" she challenged me, as soon as the door was closed again. "Are you happy now? You can go back and report to

Marie-Claire that my father's a spaced-out zombie and he's getting worse."

"Why didn't you tell me?" I snapped back. I knew it was the worst possible time for me to lose my rag with her, but it had been building up for weeks now and I couldn't help myself. "We were supposed to be *friends*, for chrissake. We were *going out* together. And you couldn't even trust me with the fact that your father's got depression. Instead, you froze me out like . . . like a bloody *iceberg*. I . . . I . . ." I was going incoherent, that's what I was.

She stared at me, as if I'd suddenly grown two heads. Then she sat down, Jekyll turned Hyde again. Or was it the other way around? She fiddled with the mugs on the tray. "I'm sorry, Hugh." She didn't look at me. "I never realised. You're right, I *should* have talked to you. It's just that . . . well . . ." She stopped. I waited. "I *do* like you. But I just couldn't cope with any more hassles in my life."

"Thanks very much."

The silence seemed to last ten hours. Finally, she looked up again. Her green eyes were wet and lost-puppy-looking. How was I supposed to stay angry with her? "I didn't mean it like that. You've no idea what a help you were. Just by being there and not . . . not pushing me. I know how hard it's been for you . . ." (like hell she did!) "but it's just . . . I dunno . . . I'm not *good* at asking for help. I know it's crazy, everyone's always telling me I'm mad, but I *have* to do everything myself. I *have* to be in charge. Can you understand that? And, with Dad getting worse and worse, I *wasn't* in charge any more. I'm scared, Hugh," she ended in a small voice.

Well, what could I do? I got up from my chair and took her in my manly arms. And, to be honest with you, it felt great.

We did a fair bit of hugging on my part and sniffing on hers and then we started talking again. "I'm glad everything's out in the open at last," Rachel said. "And I promise things'll be better now. If you still want to see me, that is."

"Of course I do," I said. I did, too.

I sat down again and put my arm round her. She left it there. We supped our tea companionably. Ma would have been pleased – she always says that all this grabbing the nearest bottle that you see on TV is crap; what people really need in a crisis is a nice cup of tea.

Rachel sighed. "What are we going to do about Dad?"

That's tyical, that is. I'd been trying to get Rachel to share her problems with me for months. Now that she had, I was totally useless. What, I asked myself, would Ma suggest?

Thinking of Ma gave me an idea. "Listen, Rache. I know your dad doesn't want you to call a doctor. But don't you have any aunts or anything, a gran even, who could talk him into getting help?" If in doubt, pass the buck. Always a good motto.

She didn't notice that I'd only mentioned female relatives – another sign of how upset she was. "He won't see any of the family. Anyway, there aren't that many: Dad was an only child. Auntie Maeve's the only relative we have in Dublin and she did try coming round once. I don't know what he said to her, but she never came again. And Gran lives too far away."

"What about your other gran? Or your grandads?"

"They're dead. There's just Granny Wilson in Manchester."

"Oh."

"Yeah. Oh."

I hesitated. "My Ma said she'd help if she could."

"Your mother?" The old Rachel rallied a bit: "How does *she* know about our problems?"

I hugged her tighter. "I was worried about you. Anyhow, she's a social worker. She knows how to get help for people. If you're dad's as bad as . . ." I was going to say, as I'd gathered from overhearing the lads on the bus, but stopped myself in time, "as Josie says he is, then he really needs help."

"He'll get better on his own." She made it sound like a mantra. "He just needs time. I mean, we *all* miss Mum. If *we* can cope, even Alice and Conor, *why can't he*?"

I knew *I* wasn't coping. Which was probably why I kept thinking Ma was the answer. *When in doubt, run to Mammy.* "Why don't you let me ring Ma? If she's at home, she'll come round. I know she will."

"What's that?" Josie came back, without the tray. "Who'll come round?"

"Hugh's mother's a social worker. He wants her to come and sort us all out."

"That's not what . . ."

Josie sat down at the table and picked up her mug. "Why not?" she asked Rachel. "We have to do something."

"We can manage."

"No, we can't. I've been taking as much time as I can off work. And you've been missing school." Rachel shook her head. "I *know* you have. So if Hugh's mother can help, I say we ask her."

"No," Rachel whispered.

Josie sighed impatiently. "We have *tried*, Rache. We *can't* do any more."

Rachel looked . . . shattered.

"What's *really* bothering you, Rache?" I asked.

"They'll take him away," she said, so softly we could hardly hear. "They'll lock him up in Saint John of God's or somewhere. He'll hate it. And what will we tell the twins?"

"Phone your mother, Hugh," Josie told me.

I looked at Rachel.

She stared straight ahead.

"Rache?"

She still said nothing.

"Shall I ask Ma to come round?"

"Do what you want. You're going to do it anyway."

I looked back at Josie. Strong, decisive, that's me.

"Go on," she said.

So I did.

Ma came round ten minutes later. It's the first time I've seen her in her professional role and I must admit I was impressed. She sat and listened to Rachel and Josie, *really* listened, and they talked to her. Even Rachel talked.

It seemed that Mr Cross had never recovered from his wife's death. At first, he'd made an effort for the sake of his children, the twins in particular, but the strain had grown on him. He'd become so snappy and irritable that the twins had had to be kept well out of his way. And he had turned more and more into himself, leaving everything in the home to Josie and Rachel and only seeming to cope with his teaching because it, probably, held no memories of his wife. But recently, even teaching had become too much for him. (Which explained the scene in his classroom, I thought to myself. Just as well that neither Rachel nor Josie knew about *that*.)

Anyhow, Rachel and Josie both seemed more relaxed after talking to Ma – possibly it was the first time they'd ever told anyone the whole story. And then Ma went in to see Mr Cross.

"She's lovely, your mother," Josie said. "But she'll never persuade Dad to ask for help."

Like father, like daughter, I thought. Now I knew where Rachel had got her pigheaded independence from. I still had my arm around her so I gave her another hug. "Ma'll sort it out. Believe me. If she can get me to clean my room every week, not to mention cook dinner every Sunday night . . ."

(this was Ma's latest ploy: it was supposed to help me learn how to fend for myself, but it didn't take a genius to work out that the main person it helped was Ma) ". . . she can get your father to do whatever's best for him, no bother."

I was right. Ma came out from her talk with Mr Cross smiling, rang their family doctor, the doctor came round, Mr Cross agreed to see him, medicine was prescribed and an appointment was made for him to see a specialist the next day.

Ma took me home with her. "You have your uses," I told her as I leant back in the front seat of the car.

She took a hand off the wheel and ruffled my hair. "I'm so glad I meet with your approval."

Chapter 26

Anne Royall, the first crusading American woman journalist, had a leg broken in Vermont by an irate Congregationalist, was horsewhipped by a young man in Pittsburgh, and fled Charlottesville, Virginia, with a mob of students at her heels.

Rachel didn't come to school the next day. I rang her as soon as I got home.

She answered the phone herself.

"Hi, Rachel. It's Hugh!"

"Are you all right?" she asked, just as I was starting to ask it myself. But she sounded amused.

"Well, *are* you, then?" I demanded.

"Yeah. I think so, anyway. Dad went in to hospital this morning. He actually seemed quite happy to be going. And he's accepted that they're keeping him there for a few days – whatever that means."

"He probably knows himself that he needs help. How do the rest of you feel about it?" (Where did I get this Ma-speak? From Ma, of course.)

"The twins are a bit upset. I mean, they've lost Mum, now they're scared of losing Dad too. Mrs Gillespie has offered to take them for as long as Dad's away, but I'm not sure if they should be moved from home. I'm thinking of asking if I can take time off school to mind them. After all, it's nearly the end of the year and we don't have exams."

"Do you want me to come round?"

"Not tonight, Hugh. But maybe tomorrow. We could take the twins to the park or something. Give them a treat."

I hesitated. "Are you giving me the brush-off again?"

"No. I *swear* I'm not. I'm just really tired. I'd love to see you tomorrow."

Did I want to start something with Rachel again? What if she shut herself off from me, as she'd done before, if things went wrong? Did I really *need* that kind of grief? The answer was yes. "What about the zoo again?" I asked.

She laughed. "If you can bear it. And if you promise we won't bump into all the Gleeson clan there. I don't particularly want to see Creepy Chris again for some time."

I thought of asking her if she was really going to apologise to him, as Frankenstein had demanded. Rachel apologizing to anyone was difficult enough to imagine; as for apologising to *Gleeson*, there was as much likelihood of that as there was of me winning the National Lottery. I decided, however, that now was not the time to pursue this. Instead I went on to a safer subject: "Frankenstein admitted that Gleeson was – how did he put it? – under some strain. D'you think that's Head-speak for an admission that you're right and that something will have to be done about him?"

"It could be. I hope it is, anyway. If so, then at least we've achieved something. I did say the pen was mightier than the sword, didn't I?"

I grinned at my end of the phone. "Mind you, Marie-Claire's probably still going around telling everyone that he never *really* meant anything." I put on a mincing feminine voice: "We shouldn't judge him too harshly. He probably needs help. He might have all sorts of troubles at home that we don't know about." Too late, I remembered Rachel's father. Shit. I'd done it again.

But Rachel only laughed. "Marie-Claire is unique," she said. "And thank God for her. We need people who believe in the good in human beings – even if they're totally wrong."

I laughed too. "OK, then. See you tomorrow, terrible twins and all. Tell them from me that, if they don't behave, I'll throw them to the lions."

"What happened to your pacifist principles?" she asked.

"Even the most non-violent amongst us have our limits," I told her. "But with any luck, I won't have to put it to the test."

Rachel was happier than I'd ever seen her, that Saturday at the zoo. And the twins were as wild as ever. We had a great afternoon and ended up taking them to McDonald's in town for tea, which they seemed to enjoy almost as much as the zoo. In the evening Rachel and I went to the cinema. And if you're interested, yes, we did kiss again afterwards.

Josie minded them on Sunday (a new boyfriend not having turned up yet) so Rachel joined Dave, Marie-Claire and myself in Dún Laoghaire that afternoon for a walk down the pier. Again, we ended up in McDonald's afterwards. It wasn't a good weekend for my spots, that was for sure.

And then it was Monday and back to school. We met at lunch-time for the first post-Frankenstein editorial meeting of *The Door.* I was nervous, but I had decided to leave it up to somebody else to challenge Rachel about her editorial for the next edition. If she apologised for the *Swiss Valley High* strip, we were OK. If not, we would be in deep trouble. (Her apology to Gleeson would have to wait: according to the school grapevine, Gleeson hadn't turned up that morning and a supply teacher had come in instead. Was this a coincidence? No doubt we would find out soon enough.)

The meeting went as normal. We had plenty of material for the newspaper. Marie-Claire had the usual kilo of poems from Jonathan; Kerry decided to start a cookery column as some lad in second year had sent in a pile of recipes which looked interesting; Louise had left us a complete list of the sports results, as usual, and a commentary on the under-fifteen's rugby match (they had drawn with Gonzaga College – it must have been some match); and I had written up a review of the film I'd seen with Rachel (which proved that my mind was on the screen at least some of the time). So all we had to sort out was who was to take over Dave's computer corner, the *Ask Mabel* column and Brian's jokes and crosswords.

"They may have been crass at times, but they livened up the paper," Kate pointed out.

"Crass crosswords," I commented. "I like it."

"And they helped to break up the pages," Kate went on, ignoring me. She didn't usually come to meetings, preferring just to get on with her drawings and then help Rachel set the paper every Tuesday. Rachel must have asked her along today.

"I suppose I can take over the crossword," Rachel said, when no one else volunteered. "Maybe you'd do the *Ask Mabel* thing, Marie-Claire: it won't have Dave's panache. . ."

"His what?"

". . . but that might be all to the good. As for the jokes, we usually get a few sent in and we can always ask for more. Could you be responsible for them, Hugh?"

"OK." I was amazed at the transformation in her, although I should have expected it on past performance: all her troubles at home seemed totally forgotten and she was the single-minded, efficient editor again.

"Fine, then," she went on. "Get everything to me tomorrow

lunch-time at the latest and Kate and I will set it up as usual tomorrow night. OK, Kate?"

Kate nodded.

I waited for someone to mention the editorial. Nobody did. In fact, they all acted as though the meeting were over and started to pack up their things.

I would have to take the bull by the horns myself: Hugh O'Connor, matador. "I assume you've decided to drop *Swiss Valley High*?" I asked as casually as I could manage. "And what about your editorial, Rache?"

"What about it?"

"Are you going to do what Frankenstein wanted? Apologise for the cartoon because it was . . . what was it he said?"

"'Scurrilous and in bad taste'," Rachel provided. She'd obviously taken it to heart.

"Yeah," I said lamely. I was aware of the others turning back to listen.

Rachel smiled sweetly at us all. "If Mr Franklin asked Kate and myself to withdraw the comic strip, of course we'll withdraw it. And if he asked me to write an editorial, of course I'll write it," she said. "What else did you expect?"

Why was I not reassured? I left her gathering everyone's copy together and headed for my next class. I'd have to talk to her after school, I decided, and make her see sense.

Chapter 27

He had to obey his conscience: it was the only weapon he had against the injustice of the world.

Andrezij Szczypiorski: ***Beautiful Mrs Seidemann***

Marie-Claire caught up with me in the corridor.

"Hugh! Have you done anything about Rachel, yet? The two of you seemed pretty close when we met yesterday – have you found out about her father? *Is* he abusing her?"

I must have looked shocked.

"Well, *is* he? You know we talked about it before."

She was right. We had done. And I'd even wondered myself, at one time, whether . . .

"She's fine," I said shortly. "Her dad's sick, that's all."

"What do you mean, sick?"

"Just sick," I said. "He's in hospital." If Rachel wanted to tell Marie-Claire the details, it was up to her.

"Are you sure?"

"Yes. Listen, I can't stay and talk – I've a class to go to."

And I let the finer points of the life-cycle of the liver fluke fill the next forty minutes.

I thought of Marie-Claire's suspicions when I went round to

Rachel's house that evening. There was no trouble now about getting into the Cross stronghold – or about Rachel coming out to join the rest of the world. It was a relief to know that it was only her father's depression that had kept her and Josie tied to the house.

It's funny how we always think the worst. I had the feeling that Marie-Claire, nice girl that she was (and she *was* genuinely nice), would almost have preferred to have had her suspicions proved true than to learn that there was nothing more sinister happening in the Cross family than Mr Cross having a nervous breakdown.

But what if it *had* been something worse? (The part of my mind which sat in the back row and commented wondered why I had such trouble with the word 'incest'. I told it I didn't know. Except that putting Rachel alongside that word was . . . impossible.) If her father *had* been . . . abusing her, had any of us done anything which would have helped? Apart from asking her all the time how she was? Is that how people get away with it? Because we're all so afraid of interfering? Because we can't believe that such a thing can happen to someone we know?

I shook my head and rang Rachel's bell.

Alice opened the door. She threw her arms round my knees in a bear hug, nearly knocking me back down the steps – I had no trouble visualising her getting a rugby cap for Ireland in a few years time. "Rachel's in the kitchen. Conor and me are watching *Eastenders*. You can watch with us if you want."

"Thanks, Alice." I disengaged myself. "Maybe later."

Rachel was busy writing in a copybook on the kitchen table, the supper debris having been pushed to one side. She looked up when I came in. "Hugh! I didn't hear the bell."

"Alice let me in. She invited me to join her and Conor and

the riveting goings-on in Albert Square, but I took a rain-check. I hope you're duly impressed."

"They watch too much television," Rachel said, frowning.

"Don't start that. Telly is the opiate of the masses; if you want to wean the twins off it, I suggest you wait a few months."

"I know." She sighed. "I just feel guilty, that's all. Mum used to ration their viewing and Josie and I let them watch anything, just for the peace."

"So? They won't die from it." I squinted at her copybook. She closed it quickly and put her arm across it.

"Aha, secrets!" I said. "Love letters to a rival, is it? Should I be jealous?"

"It's nothing. Just some work I was doing."

"It wouldn't be your editorial for the next edition of *The Door,* would it?" I asked craftily.

She blushed. "It's nothing," she repeated.

I grabbed the copy and started to pull it out from under her arm. She grabbed it back. For a moment we tugged at it like a couple of squabbling kids. Its cover came off. Rachel was left with the cover and I had the rest.

I moved out of her reach before I opened it, but she seemed to have given up the fight. She waited for me to read what she'd written.

I read.

In my first editorial for this newspaper I said that *The Door* was going to be a crusading newspaper. Well, we have crusaded - for all sorts of things. And I hope that, for some of you, we've opened a door.

Last week a door was firmly closed. The door of artistic freedom. We have been told what we have a right to print or, more precisely, what we MAY NOT print on pain of punishment. This is not only censorship, it is bullying plain and simple.

"The darkness is ticking, the wind is hollow, nothing is there." We tried to make a draught and instead we have been asked to apologize to the school, and to one member of staff in particular, for revealing an unpalatable truth.

If the school and that teacher believe that we honestly owe them an apology, they can have it. So, Mr Gleeson, if you believe that you can be recognised in the character of Lecherous Larry in the *Swiss Valley High* strip, and that your behaviour is as bad as his, then we apologize for making it so obvious. But we hope that you, in turn, will apologise to the women in this school.

That was as far as it got.

"Wow," I said. "Strong stuff."

"So?" She looked at me challengingly.

"Very strong."

"Is that all you can say?"

"You do realise that, if you print what you've written there, they'll lock you up and throw away the key?"

"So?" she asked again. "That's a risk writers have to take. Look at Socrates and Salman Rushdie."

I preferred not to. As I remembered it, Socrates had been forced to commit suicide and Salman Rushdie had been under a death threat for years. Not my idea of fun.

"What about your dad?" I asked.

"What about him?"

I hesitated, and then went ahead: after all, Rachel believed in honesty and honesty was probably the only thing that would make her see sense. "How do you think he'll like his daughter being expelled from school?"

She didn't reply, but I noticed her hands clench on the edge of the table.

I left it to sink in and started to clear away the dishes. Ma *would* have been surprised.

Eventually, Rachel turned round. "Hugh?"

I didn't know what to say, so I said nothing. And ran hot water into the sink.

"What am I going to do?" She was the vulnerable Rachel again, the one I wanted to act Sir Galahad with.

I forced myself to stay where I was – up to my elbows in soapsuds. "*You* have to decide. Nobody can do it for you."

She sighed. "You're right, of course. Dad's got enough problems. If I get into trouble at school, it'll just worry him more. *He has to get better*."

"I know."

"But . . ." She shook her head so violently that her tawny hair flew all round her face. "I can't give in to Franklin either. Or let Gleeson get away with it. I just *can't* let them win!"

I felt like sighing too. Rachel was far too high-minded for her own good. "You're going to have to compromise, Rache. One way or another. Remember that parable from *Aesop's Fables* or whatever, the one about the oak tree being blown down by the gale but the reed bending and surviving the storm?"

She actually smiled. "You're a bundle of surprises at times, Hugh."

"Blame Ma," I said modestly.

"*How* can I compromise, though? How can I stick to my principles and still keep Frankenstein happy?"

"Do you want me to work on an editorial with you?"

"No," she said slowly. "I got myself into this, I ought to be able to get myself out of it. But if you finish washing the dishes, I'll dry."

I kissed Rachel and left once the dishes were done: she said she needed space to get her thoughts in order.

I only hoped she would see sense.

Chapter 28

No one can make you feel inferior unless you consent.
Eleanor Roosevelt

Rachel refused to say anything about her editorial on Wednesday at lunch-time, but she munched her salad like a rabbit who's discovered a whole new lettuce field. She reminded me of a kid who's hidden a whoopee cushion on her gran's rocking-chair and is just waiting for granny to sit down. I found it difficult to enjoy my macaroni.

The last period of the day finally ended and I rushed down to the office. Rachel and Marie-Claire had already started photocopying. I looked at Rachel's editorial.

This may be my final editorial, I read, and you may be reading the last issue of *The Door*. If so, sorry folks - and thanks for being such loyal readers. But perhaps it will be allowed to go on under new editorship. I certainly hope so.

I feel I don't have a choice. The motto we adopted for this newspaper was "Go out and open the door!" If, at the first draught, we bang it closed again, we're not doing anyone a favour, let alone being true to ourselves.

The door which the powers that be want closed is the one which opened on to the whole subject of sexual harassment.

We dealt with this subject by placing it in a fictitious school, but it happens in schools, workplaces, even homes all over the country. What we were hoping to do was to highlight the abuse of power, the bullying of the weak by the strong.

Nobody needs to be a victim. Stand up for yourselves and shout NO!

Which is why I am shouting NO! now. I will not apologise for the *Swiss Valley High* strip. Teachers like Lecherous Larry exist, although bullies don't have to be teachers. Suzie didn't have much of a choice - no one believed her and she had to leave the school. But times will change. And the more people talk about these issues, the quicker that change will come.

I am glad that we printed *Swiss Valley High*. I do not feel it was either scurrilous or in bad taste and I will not apologise for telling the truth. But I do apologise if I have hurt anyone inadvertently, and we have decided that the strip has now ended. I hope it has achieved its purpose and has made people think.

"Go out and open the door," Miroslav Holub said. "If there's a fog, it will clear."

Let us hold on to that belief.

"Well?" Rachel asked.

I read it again.

Kerry and Kate came in.

"Is that Rachel's editorial?" Kerry asked. "Can we see it?"

I handed the spread across to her. She looked at it, a puzzled frown gathering, as they say, on her brow. "I don't get it," she told Rachel. "But then, I didn't understand your first editorial either. Have you apologised to Mr Franklin or not?"

Kate took the paper from her and cast her eye over it.

"What do you think, Hugh?" Rachel asked.

"It's very clever. We'll just have to see if you get away with it."

"I think we will," Kate said, looking up. "It's brilliant. There's no way Franklin can object to what you've written: they're all sentiments he'd have to go along with as headmaster of a progressive school. And you have apologised to Gleeson, in a sort of a way. Congratulations."

Rachel glowed.

We finished photocopying and collating the paper.

"OK," I said as the last copy was folded and placed on top of the pile. "That's that. Now we just have to wait till tomorrow and see."

The four of us went out that evening to the cinema. The *Forum* was showing an American courtroom drama and an Australian comedy.

"Let's go to the comedy," Marie-Claire suggested. "I don't feel like anything serious tonight."

"Wise move," Dave said. "Especially as some of us may find ourselves in the dock tomorrow."

"Do you really think so?" Marie-Claire looked worried again.

"Nah," I said, with more conviction than I felt. "Kate was right. There's nothing Franklin can do without looking as if he's changed his mind about what he's always telling us: that what he wants Monkscross to produce is caring, public-spirited citizens who have learnt to think for themselves."

Rachel refused to discuss it when I saw her home after the film. "Leave it till tomorrow, Hugh. We'll see what happens then."

Chapter 29

What we call the beginning is often the end
And to make an end is to make a beginning.
The end is where we start from.
T S Eliot: *Little Gidding*

All's Well that Ends Well
Shakespeare

We waited all the next day for the call to Frankenstein's office. It didn't arrive.

The end of the week came, the weekend, the next week – and still nothing happened. We began to relax.

"Maybe he's taking legal advice," Dave suggested. "Deciding whether the death penalty's OK to use on militant feminist journalists."

"Bullying is not a feminist issue," Rachel told him. "It concerns *all* of us."

"You ought to know."

"What do you mean by that?"

"Nothing."

"Come on. That's not the first time you've made insinuating remarks. Are you saying I'm a bully?"

Dave just gave her a look.

There was an embarrassed silence. Then Rachel appealed to me: "I'm not a bully, am I, Hugh?"

Did I chicken out? Or did I stick with this new spirit of honesty at all times, no matter what? I went for the difficult option – maybe Rachel *had* changed the world, or me at least. "I don't think you mean to be, Rache, but some people are kind of, well, frightened of you."

"Terrified's more like it," Dave corrected me.

"But *why*?" She seemed genuinely amazed.

I waited for someone else to jump in with a helping hand, but nobody did. So I blundered on. "You can be a bit rough at times. You know. Like, well, you don't exactly suffer fools gladly, do you?"

She bit her lip.

"Don't listen to them, Rache," Marie-Claire said. "They're just slagging."

"No, they're right." She thought for a moment and then she grinned, the old self-confident Rachel again. "OK. I promise I'll work at being more tolerant. As long as you lads do the same."

"Us?" Dave acted astounded. "We're the most tolerant men in the school, Hugh and myself. Everyone knows that."

"Hmm." Rachel smiled at him. "The only person I know who's *really* tolerant is Marie-Claire. And she would have to be to put up with you."

"Watch it, Cross. Stay out of my love life."

Marie-Claire linked arms with both of them. "Will the two of you ever stop quarrelling? It's a beautiful day, Mr Franklin seems to have forgotten about the newspaper, Mr Gleeson hasn't shown his face this week . . ."

"God's in his heaven all's right with the world," I ended for her.

The year's just about over now.

Rachel, Kate, Louise, Marie-Claire and Kerry continued working on the newspaper, with myself being, for a time, the only male on the editorial staff. I rather enjoyed my position as sultan of the harem but, sadly, it didn't last. A few weeks after Rachel's famous nail-your-colours-to-the-mast editorial, Jonathan, the prolific poet who had been sending in reams of stuff every week to Marie-Claire, joined *The Door*.

Jonathan's arrival did more than provide another male on the newspaper. (Rachel, the equal-opportunity employer?) It chucked a spanner – or a few million poems? – into the affair, if you could call it that, between Dave and Marie-Claire. Marie-Claire found she had a lot in common with Jonathan and that she hadn't really a lot in common with Dave (something we could have told her months ago). The longer she and Jon worked together, the friendlier they became: more a case of togetherness makes the heart grow fonder than of the absence that's supposed to do the trick.

I could sympathise with that. After all, it was only after I'd worked with Rachel, first on the play and then on the newspaper, that I'd begun to see her as more than just a fellow pupil.

Dave, on the other hand, was not amused. "How *can* she?" he moaned. "I mean, it's not as if he has anything going for him. He's a dweeb. He writes *poetry*."

"You write songs."

"Exactly. And she dumps *me* for *him*."

His broken heart took about a fortnight to mend. By then he'd found a new drummer to replace Gary, the drummer's girlfriend was a singer and liked his songs, and he had decided that they were going to win the Battle of the Bands at the end of term and go on from there to conquer the world. I don't know about music being the food of love but, for Dave, it's certainly a great substitute.

Fortunately, I don't need a substitute. I still have Rachel. Mind you, being in love with Rachel isn't always easy: she's still expects everyone to be as idealistic as herself and it's getting to the stage where I would *kill* for a piece of red meat. But she's much more relaxed now, especially since their family doctor arranged for them all, including the twins, to see some counselling woman (not Ma) who seems really nice.

Soon after Mr Cross was taken into hospital, Mrs Gillespie started to come in every day to help with the housework, mind the twins after school and cook the evening meal for them all: what Mr Gillespie thought of this, I didn't ask. And Mr Cross is apparently making great progress and has been home now two weekends in a row, and should be allowed out soon, for good. He doesn't intend to go back to teaching until after the summer. And neither does Gleeson, apparently. He's on a sabbatical, or so we've been told. So Rachel won after all.

Thanks to Mrs Gillespie, Rachel's not tied to the house any more but this has turned out to be a mixed blessing: she's involved in so many causes, I sometimes feel I have to queue up to get her attention. I'm still going out with her, though, and still enjoy her company. Most of the time, anyway.

So that's that. Transition Year's almost over. *The Door* is going from strength to strength and looks like becoming a must for future Transition Years – unless Rachel keeps it on for the rest of her school career. I wouldn't put it past her.

The year was certainly an experience for us all. By and large, I suppose, it was positive.

Like I said at the beginning, Ms Blenchley, we learnt a lot.

Also by Poolbeg

Circling the Triangle

by

Margrit Cruickshank

Stephen's life is a mess: his allowance is tied up for the next two years, he's facing permanent grounding at home and expulsion from school, no one appreciates the music he composes and the girl he loves treats him like a dodgy bit of meat the cat brought in. As he says, "I keep meaning to ask Ma if she noticed an evil fairy at my christening, putting a curse on me." When Stephen meets the mature and mysterious Vera, he thinks his problems are solved. But things get more, not less, complicated . . .

ISBN: 1 85371 137 3